**AT FIRST YOU WON'T BELIEVE IT
. . . THEN YOU WILL!**

Ten years ago, Tanis Helliwell
spent a summer in Ireland living in a
cottage with a leprechaun, who
taught her not only about the
evolution of elementals (faeries,
elves, devas, gnomes, leprechauns,
and so on) but also about the
interdependence of humans and
elementals in our joint evolutionary
destinies.

This book introduces many of
the secrets of the leprechaun realm
and reflects their play, sparkle,
curiosity, mischievousness, and
fun—as well as their wisdom and
divine purpose.

According to the leprechaun,
members of the elemental race are
now seeking to link with and
become co-creators with committed
human beings who believe in the
elemental kingdom and have a
desire to assist nature in the healing
of the Earth. As well as being an
enjoyable story, *Summer with the
Leprechauns* introduces humans to
the means by which we can do this.

With the charming style and
humor of her Irish heritage, Ms.
Helliwell captures the local color
of a small Irish village and its
inhabitants while revealing her
fascinating relationship with her
leprechaun friend.

**Summer
with
the
Leprechauns**

To Keith & family,

Warm wishes & joy

Tanis &

The Leprechauns

LEPRECHAUN

"A dwarf or sprite of Irish folkore, often represented as a little old man who will reveal the location of a crock of gold to anyone who catches him."

Webster's Dictionary

"I remember those 'intimations of childhood' that said there were 'little people' watching me in the garden. As I read *Summer with the Leprechauns,* I felt all the joy and mystery of that long ago time rekindle in me. This is a magical and important book and one that deserves to become a cherished classic."

—Ann Mortiffee, singer/composer

"If you think that leprechauns are no more than quaint inhabitants of an antiquated Irish fantasy—think again. Tanis Helliwell engages 'the little people' in an important cross-dimensional exchange and documents their influential presence here and now. While offering all the delights of a real-life fairy tale, *Summer with the Leprechauns* poses some ominous considerations for our planetary future."

—Joe Fisher, author, *The Case for Reincarnation, Life Between Life,* and *Hungry Ghosts*

Summer
with the
Leprechauns

a true story

TANIS HELLIWELL

BLUE DOLPHIN PUBLISHING
1997

Published by Blue Dolphin Publishing, Inc.
P.O. Box 8, Nevada City, CA 95959
Orders: 1-800-643-0765

ISBN: 1-57733-001-3

Library of Congress Cataloging-in-Publication Data

Helliwell, Tanis,
    Summer with the leprechauns : a true story / Tanis Helliwell.
    p. cm.
    ISBN 1-57733-001-3
    I. Title.
    PR9199.3.H4449S8 1996
    813'.54—dc20   96-41441
                                                           CIP

Cover art: Lito Castro and Nikki Fudge

First printing, August 1997

Printed in Canada

10   9   8   7   6   5   4   3   2   1

Dedication

 HIS BOOK IS DEDICATED to all world servers—human, angelic, and elemental—who are working to heal the Earth and to bring love, harmony, and understanding to All Beings.

Table of Contents

Acknowledgments

LTHOUGH ONLY MY NAME APPEARS AS AUTHOR, I wish to acknowledge my indebtedness both to my leprechaun friend and to other beings who taught me about elementals. Also, a special thank you to my Irish friends who befriended me and whose identity I keep silent to ensure their privacy.

For their help in bringing this book to fruition, I thank Patrick Crean, Joe Fisher, and Jean Houston, who urged me to tell my story of the little people, and all my friends who continued to ask how the book was progressing when I hadn't even started it. Another note of appreciation to Nancy and Paul Clemens, my publishers, who believed immediately in the elementals' message and very much wanted to present it to the world.

I also acknowledge a profound debt to Nita Alvarez, Alvin Hamm, Christopher McBeath, Olga Sheean, Ellen Andersen, and Nancy Flight, whose comments made the book readable for all ages and backgrounds.

I thank Tara Cullis, David Suzuki, and Ann and Harper Graham for generously providing peaceful seaside cottages where I could write.

Lastly, I thank my mother, Margaret Helliwell, who gave me Irish blood and love of all things Irish, and whose listening to the story being read aloud polished the book like a jewel.

Preface

TEN YEARS AGO, I spent a summer in Ireland living in an old cottage occupied by leprechauns. These seldom-seen beings taught me about the evolution of elementals—the race to which leprechauns, elves, goblins, gnomes, trolls, faeries, and devas belong. They explained their interdependence with humans and urged me, through this book, to promote an awareness of how humans and elementals need to work together in healing the Earth. Although my initial experience with the leprechauns took place in Ireland, they and other elementals have, over the past ten years, become part of my ongoing life. Elementals exist throughout the world and, being able to travel in space and time, can visit humans wherever we are if we call them.

At this point the reader may have some questions about my mental stability. After all, have not most of us been taught that elementals, angels, and anything that isn't anchored in third dimensional reality does not exist? I understand this dilemma and believe that we need a well-developed critical awareness so that we can separate truth from fantasy. However, if we are open to looking, there is overwhelming evidence for the existence of elementals. A hundred years ago W.B. Yeats, in his introduction to *Irish Fairy and Folk Tales,* wrote of faeries saying, "In Ireland they are still extant, giving gifts to the kindly, and plaguing the surly." While gathering his stories, he asked Paddy Flynn, "Have you ever seen a fairy or such like?" Paddy responded, "Amn't I annoyed with them." He then told of his belief in elementals, how troublesome he found them, and then continued to recount his various true experiences.

A friend of Yeats, Diarmuid MacManus, in his book, *Irish Earth Folk,* wrote in 1959, "I am no folklorist. I am merely a historian, recording as accurately as I can various happenings of recent times." MacManus was educated at the Royal Military College at Sandhurst and served in the British army in India. He came from County Mayo, the same county where my experience transpired. His criteria in reporting incidents with elementals were these: "The central character in each incident is alive, is reliable, and is prepared to stand over it firmly. And in all cases the incidents are well authenticated and can be verified by anyone."

But it's not just in Ireland that we have elementals. Almost all cultures around the world have legends and stories about them. In Iceland a recent survey that was quoted in the *Globe and Mail,* Canada's leading newspaper, indicated that forty percent of Icelanders believed in elves and gnomes. And it's not just people from European backgrounds who maintain a belief in elementals; native cultures do as well.

The Maori in New Zealand call their oldest elementals the Children of the Mist or Patupairehe. The Children of the Mist are flaxen haired and slender and are said by Maori elders to have been in New Zealand long before the coming of their people. The Maori also believe in other kinds of elementals such as the ones they call Nanakia, who are similar to elves, associated with trees, and encountered most often in forests.

I also have had too much "proof" in my life for the existence of these beings to deny their reality. I remember the first time I realized that I saw and heard things that most people don't. As a child I lived in many worlds simultaneously and was aware of voices on the wind and elemental beings glimpsed out of the corner of my eye. At that time I was unaware that others did not see and hear these beings, and so I never questioned or spoke of it. It wasn't until I was six or seven that I became aware that I was open in a way that most people weren't. This realization hit me one day as a shock.

I was walking to school with two girlfriends. One of the girls liked me and the other one didn't. The one who didn't like me kept saying nice things to me out loud, but in her thoughts she was wishing that I wasn't there.

Hurt, I said to her, "Why are you saying one thing and thinking another?" I then repeated verbatim the words that she had been thinking.

Both girls looked at me, terrified. The girl who had the nasty thoughts stared at me with both fear and hatred. The other girl, who up to then had liked me, was now frightened of me and thought I was dangerous. It was then that I understood that other people don't hear what's being thought; they only hear what's being said. And I knew simultaneously that neither girl wanted me as a friend.

Shaken, I decided that night to test my parents to see if they could hear my thoughts. During dinner I said one thing and then thought exactly the opposite to see if they would notice. To my huge disappointment, I immediately realized that my parents could hear only my words.

I decided at that moment that if I were to be accepted by other people, I would have to be like them. To do this I erected a screen so that I could not hear what others thought. Unfortunately, at the same time I closed myself to the voices and sights that had filled my childhood with wonder and magic.

I don't think my story is unique. I think many children see elemental beings—like faeries and elves—and that many of these beings are the "special" friends that their parents think their children imagine. The story of Peter Pan holds incredible attraction for children because it illustrates their connection to the magical world of elementals and the message that as adults they will have to forfeit this connection. Still, some people as adults remain open to see and hear angels and elementals. These people are called mystics or clairvoyants and it is my belief that a great many more of us can open to hear and see again as we did when we were children.

I was in my early twenties when I opened to other realities again. At that time I started meditating, which seemed to signal to the universe that I was ready to lower the screen and understand my "gifts." Within two weeks, two human beings in the spirit world appeared to assist me.

My inner journey of working with spiritual beings to develop consciousness spanned fifteen years, but I seldom spoke of it and only then to friends that I trusted. I was fortunate during that time to find a career that enabled me to use my "intuition" legitimately. In Toronto I conducted a private therapy practice specializing in personal transformation. For sixteen years I worked with individuals who were searching for deeper meaning, their soul's purpose, and who wished to discover their true gifts so that they could contribute more to the world. I also offered workshops internationally where I taught people how to develop the qualities that I had acquired naturally. My focus was always on teaching others to develop their abilities to perceive other realities, rather than to operate as a medium or psychic for them.

In 1976, in my continuing quest to ground myself in third dimensional reality, I became an organizational consultant and for twenty years have offered seminars to government, business, and educational institutions. I chose to teach topics such as Managing Stress and Change, Take Your Soul to Work, and Creative Thinking, which both allows me to help people to develop their intuition and gives me an outlet to use my mystical gifts.

So now back to the elementals! Until meeting the leprechauns I had not communicated consciously with elementals since my childhood. My path throughout my working life had been to understand how to develop "human" consciousness. It was the leprechauns and other elementals who taught me about their evolution and how humans and elementals need to work together at this time to assist both our evolutions.

The central purpose of elementals, according to the leprechaun, is to work with natural laws to create a world of beauty and diversity. Elementals help flowers to bloom, trees to grow, and even our human bodies to live. But they do more than that. They also catalyze fun, sparkle, and mischievousness in humans, stimulating their creativity and their appreciation for beauty in all the arts.

You may interpret *Summer with the Leprechauns* in a variety of ways. You might believe that leprechauns are merely the stuff of folklore, with no basis in reality. If so, I wish you an enjoyable and amusing read of my "faery tale."

Others, while never having seen leprechauns or faeries, are convinced they exist and are interested in learning more about them. For you, this story provides insights into these mystical beings, explaining their way of life and their gifts, and hopefully answering most of the questions you would like to ask.

The third group is harder to define. These people feel called to work with nature to help heal the Earth. It is my hope that you will find tools in this story to help you become a co-creator with elementals who are looking for committed humans with whom to work.

If you find *Summer with Leprechauns* enjoyable in any of these ways, I consider the book a success. We need fun and laughter to sweep away the depressing thoughts too often found in our world. Also, learning more about the elemental race, with whom we share this planet, will inspire us to change our beliefs and actions that harm both our world and theirs.

Tanis Helliwell
January 1997

CHAPTER ONE

Meeting
the Leprechauns

HERE COMES A TIME IN MOST PEOPLE'S LIVES when they harken
to a call of the blood. Their ancestral roots start pulling
them back to where they, or their parents, originated. In
my case, those roots were in Ireland.

My story started in Toronto, Canada. My personal relationship
of sixteen years was ending. The house was up for sale. My career
was ebbing and I was yearning for deeper meaning in life. I felt
drawn to go into retreat, and Ireland beckoned. At the same time
this was happening, a friend of mine was going to Ireland and I
asked her if she could find me a retreat place. I wanted a little
cottage, somewhere away from towns and villages, where I could
sit and meditate for the summer.

I had a goal in mind: to become enlightened. I'd read in various
spiritual books that, if you gave up attachments and committed
yourself to a spiritual path, you became enlightened. I had given up
my home, family, and career, and I could think of nothing else to
which I was attached. Obviously, I qualified.

Two months later my friend Elizabeth returned from Ireland,
eager to see me. She told me that throughout her travels she had
asked people if they knew of a peaceful countryside cottage for
rent. However it wasn't until her last night in Dublin, while eating
dinner with an old friend, that something turned up. Her friend

volunteered that he knew of a cottage that would be available for the summer. It was on Achill Island on the west coast of Ireland.

Within two weeks, having said good-bye to my old life, I was on the plane to Dublin. I knew that the house in Toronto would be sold and that Bill, my companion, would have started a new life by the time I returned.

I arrived in Dublin at the dawn of a business day and went to see the owner of the cottage to pay the rent and get the key. Mr. Davidson was a middle-aged, relatively successful British businessman who had worked for a long time in Ireland. Polite and reserved, he motioned me to a chair.

"Mr. Davidson," I started, careful to observe the European protocol of using last names, "how long has your family had the cottage?"

"Twenty years, but we only use it during the summer. It's vacant the rest of the year but we have a caretaker, a neighbor, Mrs. O'Toole, who sees to its care. I've told her that you're coming and she'll have the door unlocked for you."

He paused, cleared his throat, and said, "Unfortunately, I have some bad news. Within the last two weeks, the cottage has been sold."

My heart sank as he continued, "Still, the good news is that I've told the new owners that they can't have it for a month, as I had promised it to you. But after a month you're going to have to look for something else."

I sat there, stunned. I couldn't believe how quickly the circumstances of my retreat were changing, and seemingly not for the better. Two possibilities leapt to mind. Either I needed only one month to become enlightened, or there were going to be some twists and turns that I hadn't anticipated. I suspected that the latter was the most probable and that the path to enlightenment was not going to be as easy as I had hoped.

Remembering my British manners, I shook hands and thanked Mr. Davidson for giving me the cottage for a month. Heart beating with anxiety, I left his office, flagged down a cab, and headed for the bus station. The clock was ticking; within an hour I had boarded a bus bound for Achill Island in County Mayo.

We drove from city to town, town to village, village to country. The scenery became more desolate, more rugged. By the time we arrived in County Mayo, the hills were bare and rocky. The higher hills had been slashed open by farmers and local people who had cut the peat from their family plots. Approximately five hours after leaving Dublin, the bus driver pulled over at the bottom of a country lane and gestured to a hill in the distance.

"That's where you'll find the cottage," he said.

How uncanny, I thought, that a driver from Dublin would know the cottage I was seeking. I hadn't as yet learned about the highly efficient Irish grapevine.

I hoisted my pack onto my back. It was laden with sheets and clothes for the cool Irish summer. Dusk was approaching as I started up the lane, my anxiety increasing with each step.

Where would I go in a month when my time here ran out? What would I find at the cottage? Had I misconstrued the reason for coming to Ireland? And why was I always second-guessing every decision I made and worrying about the future—as I was doing right this minute?

After a half-hour walk, I came to a small, white cottage with a slate roof and a blue door surrounded by a white fence. The cottage matched Mr. Davidson's description, so I opened the gate and walked up to the door. I was surprised to see that it was ajar and called out, "Hello, anyone home?" No one answered, so I tiptoed in.

There was a fire blazing in the hearth. I let the pack drop to the floor and sat down on the nearest chair. As my eyes grew accustomed to the darkening room, I slowly took in my surroundings. There was a pile of peat beside the hearth and a bellows standing nose-down beside it. In front of the hearth was a saggy old green couch and, behind that, a large wooden table with six very sturdy chairs. To my left was a small empty room, obviously not used, and to my right was a door through which I could see a window and wardrobe, suggesting a bedroom. Behind me was a tiny kitchen which served double duty as an entrance way.

Since entering, I had felt as if I was intruding on someone's home, as if someone had left for a few minutes but would soon return to discover me. I tried to push this feeling aside, but more and more I was convinced that I was being watched. More accustomed to the fading light, my eyes swung over to the corner from which these vibrations emanated. I was shocked to find four people watching me: a small man, a small woman, and two children. I froze in place, not breathing. I've walked into someone's home, I thought, but what strange clothes they're wearing. My God, they're not human! Within milliseconds I concluded that I was in a haunted cottage. SHIT, I thought, with mounting hysteria.

Before I could proceed along this line of thinking, the little man addressed me.

"We've lived in this cottage for a hundred of your years and we're willing to share it with you, but we have some conditions."

His appearance belied the authority of his words. He was no more than four feet tall and was dressed in an old-fashioned, buttoned-up green jacket that ended at his waist. It fit tightly over a fully rounded tummy. Brown trousers, cut off at the knee, extended down to thick leggings, which were inserted into large clog shoes—larger, by all standards, than his feet had the right to be. And completing this strange attire was a gigantic black top hat.

The two boys were miniature versions of their father, minus the protruding stomach and top hat. They were fidgeting, obviously trying to behave but wanting to be somewhere else doing something different.

The little woman was dressed in a full skirt down to the floor, underneath from which peeked the same style clogs of her husband. She had on a hat that reminded me of those worn by the New England pilgrims, which seemed too large for her head. Her red hair was drawn back in a bun, but pieces refused to be confined and were busy falling down even as I looked. She was having a hard time keeping her hands still and kept wringing them, then putting them behind her back; next she'd smile at me and then, looking at her husband, she'd remove the smile and attempt to look serious.

The little man composed his face into a look of forced patience while he waited for me to respond to his offer. I was thrown off balance. Still, I had the feeling that some unexpected opportunity was awaiting me—something unlooked for but precious. I responded, matching his serious tone.

"What are the conditions?"

"We're willing to strike a deal," he countered, seemingly relieved that I could speak.

"What's the deal?" I asked defensively. I was beginning to suspect that the "we" was really an "I," and that the little woman and children were there merely as backup.

"Well . . . you're living on a haunted lane—and not all the elementals here are friendly to humans."

"Excuse me," I said, wanting to make absolutely sure that we were talking the same language, "but what do you mean by 'elementals'?"

"You humans," he said impatiently, "call us gnomes, goblins, dwarfs, faeries, elves, and leprechauns, but we're all elementals. That's our race, just like yours is the human species. There are many kinds of humans, just like there are many kinds of elementals. Now, as I was saying, we'll protect you for the summer. I know you'll need this protection because I know why you're here."

I almost stopped him again when I heard that, but decided I'd find out in due time. He seemed to realize my attention had wavered, because he paused before continuing.

"In return, at the end of the summer," he said, "I'll ask you for a gift."

"What's the gift?"

"We'll not tell you now. We'll tell you at the end of the summer," he responded.

Somewhere in my foggy memory bank I recalled stories of humans being tricked by faeries and elves, and I was leery of striking any open-ended deal. I could say that I didn't have any choice, as this was his cottage and I had nowhere else to go, but that wouldn't have been quite true. I believe that I could have lived there physically for the summer and simply closed myself down to these little people so that I never saw them again. But what unimaginable experiences would I be shutting out at the same time? And deep down I had a feeling that he would make a fair request. It was almost as if, even then, I was trusting him, so I said, "I agree."

I remembered Robert Frost's poem, "The Road Not Taken," in which the poet is on a walk in a wood when he comes to a fork in the road and says, "And I—I took the the one less traveled by, And that has made all the difference." I felt as if the leprechaun had offered me the same option of walking down the road not taken with him. I had no idea where this journey would lead, but I knew I would regret it if I passed up this opportunity.

Our bargain concluded, the leprechaun withdrew his attention, making it clear that our conversation was over for the evening. The little woman and children had already disappeared. Exhausted, I picked up my pack and entered the bedroom. The sturdy double bed, with wooden head- and footboard, had obviously provided comfort to generations of weary bodies. Undoing the zipper of my pack, I pulled out my bed linen and made the bed. In the cupboard were several woolen blankets, all of which I added. Shivering with cold, I took off my glasses and put them on the beside table. Then I tore off my clothes, put on my granny gown, and hopped under the covers. Within minutes, I was sound asleep.

CHAPTER TWO

Mrs. O'Toole

HE NEXT MORNING WAS GLORIOUS AND SUNNY and, having skipped dinner the night before, I was starving. Tying an extra sweater round my waist—in case the weather changed—and pulling my purse over my shoulder, I set out to purchase some food for my larder. Opening the gate into the lane, I paused. Facing me was a sweeping view of fields bordered by hedgerows leading to majestic cliffs that fell straight into the sea. Far off to the right, where the lane met the sea, was a small cluster of buildings—the village, I surmised.

Breathing deeply of the clean moist air, I set off down the lane. Bordered by a ten-foot-high hedgerow, and with little drainage ditches on either side, the lane was only wide enough for one small car. Gaps in the hedge revealed beautiful brilliant patches of yellow irises and daisies in fields of lush green grass. It was hard to believe that there were dangerous elementals lurking in the lane. It was an early morning of optimism and joy and I celebrated my good fortune of having a month in a cottage in this magnificent country.

Gradually I wove my way towards the village and arrived at a crossroads that had two pubs and one general store. "Slim pickins," I thought, as I walked up to the store, pulled back a squeaky door, and entered. All eyes turned towards me and a hush fell. A stranger had arrived. I smiled and immediately started perusing the grocery section. To my relief, the normal buzz of daily chatter resumed.

Some time later, after choosing food calculated to maximize the number of meals I could prepare with the lightest load to lug back up the lane, I looked around for the place to pay. There was a man behind the counter with a white apron tied round his middle and a look of ownership about him. I sauntered over and placed my purchases before him. As he was checking out the goods, he asked as casually as he could manage, "Are ya a holiday-maker then?"

"I've rented the Davidson's cottage for the summer," I responded, not eager to give out information for town gossip, but less eager to deny him some joy in the telling.

His left eyebrow arched two inches and, looking me in the eye, he said with gravity, "Did ya not know that the Davidson's cottage is haunted?"

Thinking that ignorance was the best strategy, I responded, "Oh! Haunted by what?"

"Why, by the little people," he quickly countered. "Not only that, but yer livin' on a haunted lane. There was a caravan parked right across from yer cottage and it used to shake and rattle and all manner of things would happen with no one in it."

He probably would have gone on, given any encouragement, but this news, which confirmed my experience of the previous night, left me rattled. If everyone in town knew of these "hauntings," the elementals could not be easily dismissed. I felt dark clouds begin to sweep in over my previously sunny day. I didn't think he was trying to scare me off. It felt more like the Irish joy of telling a bit of local history, yet I sensed that he had a mischievous streak that prompted him to have a little fun unsettling the foreigner. He certainly succeeded.

I thanked him and picked up the bags to leave. I knew that, as the "American" (Canadians are not distinguished as separate by the Irish) who had rented the haunted Davidson cottage, I would be the subject of conversation at every dinner table that evening. I could just see them laying bets on my chances of lasting.

I started back up the lane, weighed down by both the supplies and the information. Now, as I walked by the hedgerows, I was steely and frozen, imagining lurking beings waiting to jump out at me. Arriving at the cottage, I heaved a sigh of relief. Entering, I unloaded the groceries, ate a hurried brunch, and then set about making the place feel like home. The leprechauns were nowhere to be seen, nor was I looking for them. Perhaps they had decided to give me some time to get accustomed to my surroundings. Whatever the reason, I was grateful to be left alone.

entrance gate and view from cottage

Through furniture rearranging, setting up a meditation altar, and flower-gathering, the time passed quickly. Lengthening shadows announced the sun's descent and it was time to light the fire. Picking up four pieces of turf, I arranged them one on top of the other, being careful to leave space for air. Taking the wooden matches from the mantel, I struck one and placed it under the turf. Nothing happened. Again and again I tried, without success.

Annoyed, I grabbed the new diary I'd bought to document my summer of enlightenment, and tore out several blank pages. Placing them carefully under the turf, I tried again. The paper caught immediately. Congratulating myself, I sat back on the couch and watched while the flames died down and down and went out.

I would have preferred not to need a fire. After all, it was summer. But it didn't take me long to learn that summers in Ireland and in Canada bore little resemblance to each other. The cottage was so cold and damp that, even on the warmest day, the temperature inside never rose above 62 degrees. Shivering, and fresh out of fire-starting ideas, I looked up and saw a head appear at my gate. It was covered in a kerchief with straggly gray hair falling out the front and sides. A well-worn working hand reached around, unlatched the gate, and swung it open. The body attached to it was covered in a dirty blue-gray raincoat held together by two buttons. With every step the coat flared open, revealing a faded floral dress and a slip that hung down unevenly below the hem. In her muddy "wellies," she strode purposefully towards the door, holding in her right hand a walking stick almost as tall as herself.

I hastened to the door and was greeted by twinkling mischievous eyes, and a smile with enough teeth missing to keep a dentist in business for a year.

"I be Mrs. O'Toole," she said, and her eyes veered right to the cold hearth, where the remnants of my failed attempts told all.

I stepped aside and without another word she went straight to the fireplace. Carefully putting the sods of turf aside, she brushed the paper ashes away and, one by one, replaced the sods in a tent-like formation. Then she struck a match under the canopy and, within minutes, the turf was ablaze.

That doesn't look too difficult, I thought, witnessing the procedure. I'll manage it with no problem tomorrow. I was innocent that first day in the cottage. I still believed that I could control my environment and, using my own free will, take the necessary steps to consciousness. Little did I know that day that I would never once be able to light the turf, and that Mrs. O'Toole would rescue me at the same time every day. This first day, although grateful for her help, I still resented the intrusion. I had planned days and weeks of silence and meditation, and my plan had been disrupted first by the leprechauns and now by her. I didn't know then how much I would come to welcome her visits.

"Would you like a cup of tea?" I offered as she, uninvited, sat herself down on the couch.

"Aye," she replied.

Excusing myself, I hurried to the kitchen to put on the water and busily got out cups and biscuits. The Davidsons had left some sugar that had solidified from the damp and I chiseled some of it free with a knife and put it in a cup. All ready, I reentered the living room. Mrs. O'Toole was sitting calmly, gazing into the fire.

I sat down at the other end of the couch and, as there was no table, carefully put the tray on the floor in front of me. Mrs. O'Toole was still gazing at the fire, seemingly in no hurry to start a conversation.

"Would you like your tea now?" I asked after a few minutes. Irish people usually like their tea strong, so I had let it brew a bit.

"Aye," she replied.

"Sugar?" I invited.

"Aye."

"I'm sorry I don't have any milk," I said.

"I'll bring some tomorrow from the coos."

Those words were my first indication that Mrs. O'Toole and I were going to see a lot of each other. My previous expectations started dissolving at that moment and I decided to attempt to stay open to whatever the universe was providing. I didn't mention my planned silent retreat. Instead I asked, "Would you like a biscuit?"

"Aye," was her answer. We sat there sipping our tea and munching in silence. Her presence was comforting. She was cozy, like the fire burning in the hearth. I settled back into her warmth. A couple of times I tried to start a conversation.

"Where do you live Mrs. O'Toole?"

"Up the lane."

"Which way would that be?"

"On the way to the village."

"What do you do up there?"

"We've a farm."

Her tea finished, Mrs. O'Toole stood up and said, "I'd best be goin' now," and, stick clicking across the wooden floor, she walked out the door. I was left with questions unanswered. Would she fit into my idea of the summer? How often would she come?

CHAPTER THREE

Leprechaun Evolution

I AWOKE THE NEXT MORNING to find dozens of eyes peering at me. Elementals of every description filled the room and they watched intently as I bolted upright.

"Yer right, she sees us, she sees us," a particularly ugly one, with warts all over his long hooked nose, squealed with delight. His immense gnarled hands grabbed the footboard as he hauled himself forward for a better look. Even without my glasses, I had no trouble seeing his grotesque features.

"Told ya so, told ya so," chirped the two children who lived in the cottage, as they began to dance around the room.

I felt like an animal in the zoo on display for the entertainment of the neighborhood gnomes and goblins. Furious, I screamed, "Get out. This is an invasion of privacy. This is not part of the deal." My voice blew them apart like a wind passing through grass. Some scattered out the bedroom door, some through the walls, and others simply disappeared. Only one remained—the male leprechaun who claimed to live in the cottage.

Hands clasped behind his back, rolling back and forth on the balls of his feet with eyes cast down in mock shame, he sighed, "I told them it was a bad idea but the little 'uns were all excited about having a human in the cottage so they invited in the neighbors for a look. Anyway, there's no harm done."

I remembered some of the faces at the bottom of the bed— faces which were, by human standards, grotesque and malevolent-

13

looking. I wasn't going to be mollified as easily as that and countered, "Weren't some of those," I indicated, waving my hand in the direction where the one with the warts had hovered, "the ones that hate humans?"

Eyes still averted, he continued with what I believe he took to be the expected apology, "Well, you're right of course. There were a few that live down the lane but you couldn't invite some without inviting them all. That would be causing more problems."

Unclasping his hands, apology complete, he looked at me and said in his businesslike voice, "Anyway, get up; we're going to start today." With those words he turned his back and, with dignity, sauntered out of the bedroom.

Appreciating his understanding of my need for privacy, I dressed quickly, at the same time wondering if leprechauns had a similar need. Shivering, I headed for the kitchen to put on the water for tea. He was waiting for me at the front door, impatient for me to join him.

"I'll be there as soon as I get a cup of tea," I stated, defending my desire for bodily comforts.

"I'll have one as well," he responded pertly.

"You drink tea?"

"Of course I drink tea," he replied, "but that's part of what I'm going to talk to you about. So, get us both a cup and a couple of chairs and meet me outside."

He turned quickly and walked right through the closed door. Smiling at his antics, I turned on the kettle and headed back to the bedroom for another sweater. Following the leprechaun's instructions, when the tea was ready, I carried it and the chairs outside.

The leprechaun pretended not to notice my arrival and busied himself looking at the buttercups and daisies as if seeing them for the first time. I knew intuitively that he expected me to play the role of hostess so he could play the role of guest. Amused, I very carefully arranged his chair and tea cup and courteously said, "Your tea is ready."

He looked up, nodded, and then as elegantly as he could manage, walked over and sat down, folding his hands over his ample stomach. "Let's start from the beginning," he announced, much as Yahweh might have done when he said, "Let there be light."

"I'm what you humans call a leprechaun, and my study is humans," he commenced, with an Irish lilt in his voice. "I'm being tested on my knowledge of humans, and this summer is critical."

He was like an actor playing the part of a human scholar from the last century. He was a little exaggerated and theatrical. In fact, he reminded me a bit of W. C. Fields. I managed to keep a straight face, even though I could see that, underlying his scholar pose, there was roguery and good humor—as if he was enjoying playing a part, and was especially enjoying having an audience.

"What is the test?" I inquired, eager to find out more about it.

"I've been studying humans for about a hundred of your years and I'm one of the first elementals to be engaged in this. Elementals are different from humans in that we're born into a caste and stay in it for our entire lives. But about a hundred years ago, and I can remember this, for a hundred years is the same as yesterday with us, elementals were asked if they would volunteer to study humans. I took it up. I was only young then, just coming out of my puphood."

"Who asked you?" I interrupted, becoming more and more intrigued by his story.

"I'm getting to that," he responded, not wanting to be hurried.

"You see, elementals, unlike humans, can never be creators on this planet. Humans have, from the beginning of their evolution, been training to become creators—gods-in-training if you will—and the Earth is your school. Humans have free will, which is necessary for all creators, and you're the only race on this planet, save the people of the water, that has this."

As he spoke of the people of the water, I saw an image of dolphins and, as he continued, I began to see all sorts of images relating to his words. I also began to feel things that reinforced both his words and the images. I realized that this three-dimensional communication of hearing, seeing, and feeling was giving me a much fuller and more rapid understanding than was normal for humans. As I listened, I also began to realize that in my everyday existence I received information from my environment on many dimensions and that how the leprechaun communicated was in some ways more familiar to me than the way I communicated with my fellow-humans. The leprechaun seemed to sense that his communication had triggered these thoughts and paused for a few moments before continuing.

"Elementals used to have good lives in Ireland. It's still better in Ireland than most places but gradually the space where we can live has diminished, our quality of life has shrunk, and as a race we're dying. So, a hundred years ago we were asked, by the ones who control our evolution, if we would like to study humans and attempt to learn free will while still remaining in elemental evolution. This way we could start becoming creators like humans. I'm one of the first who chose to do this."

"Are you saying that only humans and dolphins can become creators and that elementals can't? How do you evolve then?" I asked, intrigued.

"Up until a hundred years ago, the only way that elementals could become creators was to enter human evolution. Our most advanced elementals—you'd call them masters—often did this. Vincent Van Gogh was one of our elemental masters, and he could see how our world was dying, so he requested permission to enter human evolution. He wanted to learn free will so that he could help elementals. But his life was very difficult as a human because our two worlds are very different.

"Because he wanted to help elementals, he never quite separated from us. Also, he wanted to give humans the beauty of our arts and our world, but they weren't ready for it. He found it difficult to live trapped in a body that was so confined in time and space."

"Was Van Gogh totally an elemental or just partly?" I asked, trying to understand how humans and elementals could totally enter each other's worlds.

"Van Gogh, because he was so strong," the leprechaun replied, "was allowed to take almost all of his elemental essence into your world. But he was the exception. Usually, elementals are allowed to put only part of themselves into a human life. So a human could be ten percent or twenty-five percent elemental. This makes it easier for elementals to survive in the human world, but it takes much longer this way—several lifetimes in fact—for them to learn enough human qualities to become creators in our world."

"How would we recognize a human who was part elemental?" I asked, suspecting that I'd probably known some in my life.

"Such humans are often gifted in the arts," he answered, "singing and dancing and story-telling. Quite a few of them have been Irish or Welsh, and Dylan Thomas was one of them. He'd quite a bit of elemental in him."

"But how do the human and elemental parts get sorted out," I asked, "so that these beings can continue their evolution? It sounds to me like they become hybrids, not one thing or the other."

"That's exactly what happens," the leprechaun smiled, appreciating my perception. "Humans can apply to enter elemental evolution as well, but that's another topic. Anyway, until a hundred years ago, this was the only way that elementals could acquire free will to become creators but, as you can see, it was a difficult and slow process. It's a difficult life for elementals and for the humans that they meet. Human and elemental laws are not the same. Elementals don't have what you call 'morality.' We don't get married and stay sexually loyal like you humans do. So, when elementals enter human evolution, we are accused of promiscuity and disregard for others but, by our laws, we are not doing anything wrong."

"So if that was how the old system of elemental evolution worked," I said, "what is your role in the new system?"

"In my world," the leprechaun replied eagerly, "I'm a teacher of elementals who are studying humans, just as you are a teacher of humans who are studying other evolutions. In fact, in our respective worlds, our roles are very similar."

As he spoke about our similar roles, I was aware of how little I understood. All my adult life, while working with people both individually and in seminars, I had attempted to help them to see predictable patterns in both their personal development and in the consciousness of all humans. Before coming to Ireland, I thought that my understanding of and cooperation with these patterns were enough to earn me enlightenment. Now here was the leprechaun speaking of a totally new dimension—namely, the evolution of elementals—about which I knew nothing.

I was starting to wonder how much more I could take in, when he added, "You and I are both interested in helping beings to become conscious creators on this planet. I'm going to teach you about elementals this summer and you're going to teach me about humans so that I can pass my test. We're both at the same stage and we're both being tested this summer. You haven't quite got it right, you know."

"What do you mean?" I asked, slightly nettled.

"You think you're here for enlightenment, and that's true, you are, but you don't fully understand how this happens. I'm going to help you. I can't help with the human learnings of course. But I can help with the process. I'm older than you and I've learned a few things over the years."

He shifted his weight and looked down at his teacup, which was on the ground. I blinked and suddenly the teacup was in his hands and he was raising it to his lips. My gaze quickly returned to the ground and found the original teacup still where it had been. There were two identical teacups, one on the ground, and one in his hands.

"I haven't had tea at home since last summer," he volunteered. "Not since the Davidsons were here."

I was pleased to see that he was attempting to generate some camaraderie, so I asked, "Do you like living with humans?"

"It's not so much like or not like, it's the way of it now, unless you want to live under a bridge or in the barn with the coos. It's hard to find a cottage that isn't occupied with humans all the time and now cottages are going out of style. Modern houses are being built and it's just not the same. We're not made for electric heat, we're made for turf. We've been lucky with the Davidsons. They're not here much and, when they are here, their vibration is in resonance with ours. It's almost like we're having guests. We've watched the little 'uns grow and, all in all, it's been fine."

He leaned forward, placing his teacup where the other was and I watched, fascinated, as they both merged into one. His manner was so matter-of-fact that somehow this magical version of reality seemed instantly acceptable.

"Maybe I should be starting at the beginning," he said, replacing his hands on his stomach and resuming his teacher's pose. "Most humans don't see us. Humans live most of the time in the third dimension and we live about half a dimension away from you. It is easy for us to see humans as you are coarser, denser, altogether more gross, and you vibrate at a slower rate than us.

"You humans," he turned to me apologetically and said, "not you personally of course, are not able to see the lighter vibrations. You can't see humans that have died, the beings that form the clouds, and the ones that grow the trees. Elementals feel a combination of what humans call pity and disgust that you can't see these other dimensions. If you humans could raise your vibration and see these dimensions, then you would not be doing to the world what you've been doing. How could you be killing the streams and the trees if you saw the life force in them and the beings that are growing them?

"We elementals have got this theory that maybe humans have made themselves coarse and dense on purpose, so that if they can't see us and other beings, they could do as they wanted. Humans do this by eating meat, watching violent films, and generally focusing on their bodily appetites. By doing this, humans become too coarse to see elementals and all life in nature, so they can do as they like to "inanimate" matter.

We've noticed that humans have got a very strong desire to do what they want. This is the downside of free will, if you like. Beings need free will to become creators but most humans have to go through a struggle with their strong will—ego you call it—in order to harness it to what's wanted by the creator."

I sat quietly sipping my tea and listening to his words. I agreed with his insight and felt sad that so few people took the time to allow the beauty of their surroundings to affect them.

As if he sensed the change in me, he turned and said, "See how much better you feel when you relax and allow the beauty of the world to move you?"

Although I hadn't projected my thoughts, I knew that he had picked them up easily. I realized, startled, that if he wished, he could be aware of every thought I had the entire summer.

"But I don't wish," he said. "I've got a life outside of this conversation. Also, I know how touchy you humans are about privacy."

It was clear from his tone that, in some ways, he saw me and all humans as younger, and therefore less advanced, than him.

Immediately he started to giggle and soon was doubled up in laughter. Then, without speaking, he projected an image of tiny faeries with wings doing mischievous things, and I realized that he was conveying the stereotypical human image of elementals.

"Okay, okay," I said, laughing. "Both of us will have to work at eliminating stereotypes about each other's race, and we can have fun doing it."

"As I was saying about free will," he said, sober once again, "elementals have very little because we don't need it. We can manifest whatever we want because, unlike humans, we don't doubt that we can. We might play a joke on humans, or on our own kind, but it's for a bit o' fun. It's not to do what you call an 'evil' thing. Like today in the bedroom when the little 'uns brought in the others to see you. Now, what harm did that do? It didn't do any.

"You, in fact, could have done more harm when you started screaming at them. You blew them away. Now, as it happens, none of them were harmed, but humans can hurt elementals just by the force of their will and what they say and do. Humans have certainly harmed elementals by what they think. Humans have denied our existence, especially over the past hundred years and, because they don't believe in us, they don't give us energy to exist. Some elementals, without human energy going into belief in us, have snuffed out of existence. These are the ones who had the smallest wills and who needed human belief to keep going."

I was feeling terribly guilty by what I had done, not through conscious intention but through ignorance. "This is awful," I said. "I had no idea that humans had harmed elementals so much."

He paused, and I could feel him considering options, struggling to maintain the objectivity of a human scholar. "As it happens, humans have done elementals some good," he said finally. "When we saw that humans' lack of belief in us deprived us of energy, it forced some of us to take the path we're taking. We must develop our will and believe in ourselves.

"This was not the way it was meant to be originally in the scheme of things. We had our gifts to bring into the world and you had yours. Elementals' gifts are those of laughter, joy, and beauty. The gifts of humans are those of will, action, and doing. In the original plan, we were to evolve separately but in harmony to complement each other. But that's not the way it's gone over the last several hundred years. So the beings who control our evolution have changed our plan, just like they've changed yours, and now they're getting together a plan whereby we can both be creators. If elementals can work with humans, as I'm working with you, this will go much quicker. We're looking for humans to work with for the good of both our races and also for the good of the Earth."

"How can we work together?" I asked simply.

He redirected his attention towards the horizon. He didn't seem to like looking at me as he spoke, and I realized that my energy was too distracting for him. He needed to focus all his attention on what he was saying.

"There are many ways that humans can work with elementals. The first is to believe in them and to understand that they bring joy and beauty to the world. Elementals help flowers, trees, and mountains to grow. There is even an elemental that maintains your body. Just because humans can't see them doesn't mean they don't exist. There are many dimensions in which humans aren't conscious. Even elementals—although conscious of your reality and other realities—can't see all realities. But both humans and elementals can improve this ability to perceive other dimensions. When humans believe in us, it creates and strengthens the thought-forms that allow us to function and grow. This takes very little energy from you and gives us so much. If humans were to do this, more elementals would develop consciousness so that we too could develop free will to become creators. It would definitely hasten our evolution."

I was tempted to ask about thoughtforms but his intent expression discouraged me, and he continued.

"Another way of working with us is to show gratitude, appreciation, and joy for what we have created. When humans do this we can enter them so that they are fertilized and catalyzed by our essence."

Turning towards me, he added, "This is what you did a few minutes ago; remember how you felt happier?"

I nodded in agreement, opened my mouth to speak, and once again was washed back by the flow of his words. "Humans sink into themselves and think about serious things like work and duties. This makes them tighter, denser, and delays their evolution. As humans become more conscious they become lighter and more porous. Elementals can see, just by looking at humans and noticing their density, what state of evolution they're at. If humans saw the beauty in the world, this would hasten their evolution.

"Elemental evolution is the opposite from humans. When first we incarnate, we are just wisps of energy. But as we grow and develop, we become increasingly solid and dense. So the purpose of elemental evolution is to increase density."

Once again I attempted to comment on his words, only to be silenced by another stern look. I was beginning to wonder if I was ever going to get a word in edgewise.

"Two other ways we could work together," the leprechaun continued, looking at me with exaggerated patience, "is for humans to commit to working with elementals who want to work with them. Our work is to create form, to see the pattern that is in nature, and to encourage that pattern to develop. Elementals can see the pattern that is in individual humans and we can help grow you—just like we grow a tree or a flower. This will accelerate your evolution. Humans say that every person has a guardian angel, and they're right, they do. They could also have a friendly elemental.

"What humans could do for us is meditate on what elementals are doing in nature and send energy to help us to do this. Elementals can learn to use their free will by working with individual humans. If we could work together, then elementals would not have to risk entering human evolution."

With these words, he stretched his hands above his head, opened his mouth in a big yawn, and smiled at me. Relieved to have finished his lengthy monologue, he said, "That's enough for today, don't you think?" Without waiting for an answer, he stood, turned, and walked through the wall back into the cottage.

After the leprechaun's departure, I closed my eyes, relaxed back in my chair, and let the cool breeze of the Irish morning wash over me. I took a deep breath and, releasing it, allowed the impact of the morning to settle. My image of the retreat had changed radically in only two days, and I was reminded of what the leprechaun had said about elementals understanding the divine plan better than humans. Whereas elementals were learning free will, humans needed to learn how to cooperate with the divine plan. What the two races had in common was the need for a healthy balance of both aspects.

I was obviously being given an opportunity this summer to create that balance. Before coming to Ireland I had seen only one strand of my life path and how it fit with other humans. I had not seen the weave of other beings' life paths in the tapestry, and now I started to see glimpses of how we fit together as part of a greater whole.

Before coming to Ireland I had only the goal of enlightenment. My image of the process was that I would be tested in some way and I would either pass or fail. I had a tendency to view enlightenment in absolutes rather than as an evolving process, yet I knew this was antithetical to what Buddhists called the "journey without the goal." Perhaps this summer was the opportunity for me to experience a journey without worrying about the goal. Who I thought I had been was in the past, and now I was in Ireland to see who I really was.

CHAPTER FOUR

The Essence of Food

Y STOMACH WAS GRUMBLING FOR FOOD, so I pulled myself out of the chair and went inside. As I dropped two slices of bread into the toaster, I felt eyes on my back. I turned and discovered the entire leprechaun family ravenously eyeing my breakfast.

"Do you eat toast?" I asked.

"We certainly do!" asserted the elder leprechaun, beaming his most charming smile in my direction.

I picked up the bread knife and cut four more slices of bread, mentally calculating the cost of feeding five people—instead of one—over the month.

"No need to worry," I heard over my right shoulder. "We're very particular about what human food we eat."

Wondering if I could learn to have thoughts that my leprechaun friend wouldn't be able to hear, I busied myself with the toast. I was just about to ask what they would like on it when, unsolicited, came the reply, "butter and honey."

With honey pot, butter dish, and platefuls of toast on an old wooden tray, I went into the living room. The family was already seated at the table, waiting impatiently. I placed a plateful in front of each of them and sat down beside them.

"Irish soda bread. Delicious," slurred my friend, with honey dripping from his fingers. The toast was in two places: one solid piece was on the table where I'd placed it, while a second, more

25

misty one, was being held reverently in his hands and was shrinking as I watched.

I turned my gaze to the foot of the table where the female
leprechaun sat. She caught my eye and put her hand over her mouth
to stifle the giggles that were emerging. Obviously she found this
little scene amusing. Seeing how it must have looked from the
leprechaun's perspective, I began to laugh until I realized, by the
uncertain look in their eyes, that the strength of my emotion was
overwhelming them. I was reminded of what my leprechaun friend
had said about my anger being strong enough to hurt them, and I
quickly muted my tones. The little woman immediately relaxed.

Sitting across from me were the two "little 'uns." By human
standards they would have been between five and nine, but I knew
that, as elementals, they could be much older. Nonetheless, they
both looked and acted like smaller versions of human children that
age. Unlike the adults, they seemed to be unable to lift the toast
securely and were busy sniffing it on their plate while it hopped up
and down.

Again I smiled, thinking of the fun human kids would have if
they could make their food move using their minds. Leprechaun
children could teach human kids to levitate food, and the humans
could teach the leprechauns the concentration necessary to keep
the image steady. I caught the male leprechaun watching me and
knew that he was following my thought, and that I had correctly
determined a way for each race to assist the other. I also realized
that the secret friends that human children have are often elementals, because children are still open to the elemental world.

"Are they," I inquired, nodding towards the children and little
woman, "going to be teaching me as well?"

"Not directly," the leprechaun replied. "She's very silly and
the little 'uns are too young to hold a thought long enough for you
to understand what they are thinking."

I looked at the little woman to see her reaction to being called
"silly." She never seemed insulted; in fact, she smiled at me before
returning her attention to the toast in her hands that had almost
totally dissolved.

"How do you do that?" I asked, pointing towards the toast. She started to giggle and the male leprechaun answered for her. I could see that he was the dominant partner and tried not to judge their relationship by my human standards of equal relationships between male and female.

"Elementals don't eat the being, they eat the essence of the food. The closest way for you to understand is to say that we breathe in the essence. This is the way we sustain ourselves. We are very particular, by human standards, about what we eat. Many of your foods are repulsive to us. We don't kill any being to eat. We don't eat coos, sheep, chicken, or fish."

I could see disgust rising in him as he spoke and knew that if I held that image for long enough, I might become a vegetarian. "Well, there are always salads," I thought.

"No there aren't. Lettuce is alive," he continued, shooting me an image of a very live lettuce being pulled up by its roots by a heartless human. I could almost hear the death screams. This was particularly poignant for me as lettuce was one of my favorite foods, and I often congratulated myself for eating products so low down on the food chain. I hadn't eaten pork for eight years, and ate beef and chicken only occasionally.

"What do you eat then?" I asked defensively, convinced that it would be impossible for humans to exist if they ate like elementals.

"We eat milk, butter, grains, and anything that isn't killed," he responded with a touch of superiority. "Human evolution will go in this direction. Have you noticed that humans don't eat as many coos as they used to. Now you are eating more chicken and fish. After a while people won't even eat these and will focus more on vegetables and fruits. This is necessary for your body to become lighter, if you are to evolve. There will be a time, in your distant evolution, that you will absorb the essence of food like we do."

"Could you be more specific about the kinds of foods you eat?" I asked, wondering if a lighter diet this summer would hasten my enlightenment.

"Any kind of grain would be fine, so you could make us porridge in the morning," he said, smiling at his own not-so-subtle hint. "We quite like oats but we're not keen on corn as it's not from Ireland. Humans must learn to eat foods that agree with their body—foods that come either from where they or their ancestors were born. Elementals restrict their diet to locally-grown foods, rather than foods that come from far away. They nourish us better."

"So would you eat a potato?" I asked, thinking of the Irish love of potatoes.

"Aye, because we don't destroy the potato being for the potato."

"But how do you avoid destroying the plant?" I inquired.

"We go to the potato plant and ask it to please give us one of its children. The plants decide amongst themselves which potatoes would be suitable for us and then we go into the earth and pull out the essence of the potato that the plants have selected."

As he spoke, I remembered times when I had picked beans and berries and asked the plants for permission. Sometimes I'd heard yes and sometimes no. When I heard no, I never proceeded.

"That's just the way elementals do it," said the leprechaun, tapping into my thoughts. "And this is the procedure all humans should use in gathering food."

"As for butter and milk," he said, continuing with his list of "permissible" foods, "the coos give us this freely. When it comes to honey, we are the bees' best friends. They are happy to provide for us, as we help grow the beautiful flowers that give them pollen."

"Do you drink alcoholic beverages?" I asked, with a smile, recalling stories of inebriated leprechauns.

"Well, of course," he replied, with a conspiratorial wink. "Our favorite alcohol is mead, which is made from honey. In the olden days, humans drank mead at weddings. Elementals really looked forward to going to weddings and parties so they could sing and dance and drink mead. There's not much mead about now so we make do with Guinness, and occasionally wine."

"How do you get humans to give you a drink, when humans can't see you?" I asked, certain some trick must be involved.

"Well, there are two ways of doing it," he proceeded. "If we've got a good relationship with the human, they set out a bowl of milk for us or pour us a glass of mead. This is the way it was up until a couple of centuries ago. Humans respected us and knew that we kept their crops healthy, and we worked in partnership together. This doesn't happen often now, so this only leaves the second option."

Somewhat shamefaced, he continued, "Now when humans pour their glass of mead, we zip in there and have some before they get it to their lips. What the human doesn't realize is that after we've drunk the essence from their glass, what's left won't taste as good to them. Immediately after doing this, we leave, as we find it repulsive to see the humans drinking the remnants of what we've already eaten."

With these words, he looked down at the pieces of toast on the table. To me, they looked identical to how they had looked when I placed them there. "If you were to eat this toast now, it would be repulsive to us. We've taken the life force from it and, if you eat it, that would be almost as bad as eating a being that you had killed—almost, but not quite."

I was still digesting his information when the leprechaun said, "Anyway, that's your lesson on food and what to eat," and with those words he nodded at me and disappeared.

The children remained seated, as did the little woman. She looked like she wanted to say something, while the children kept glancing at me and fidgeting. I had the impression that they were trying to concentrate and stay focused. The little woman watched me observing her children, and I could feel that she was waiting for my help in some way. I extended my aura across the table and sent a beam of focused peaceful thoughts in their direction. This immediately had an impact. The children were able to look at me for much longer without moving. I looked back at their mother just in time to catch her smile before all three disappeared.

CHAPTER FIVE

Taking the High Road

OLLOWING THE DEPARTURE OF THE LEPRECHAUNS, I threw the toast into the trash bin and put the dirty plates in the sink. Two days earlier I probably would have chosen to stay inside to meditate, but no longer. Instead I decided to spend the rest of the day on a journey without a goal. It was a rare dry day—one of the very few I was to experience that summer. Nonetheless, blue jeans and a wool sweater were necessary in order to stay warm. Being slender, I needed all the padding I could get.

Too bad, I thought, that the leprechaun couldn't arrange to transfer a few pounds of fat my way for extra warmth. While we were at it, with me being five-foot-three and him only coming up to my shoulder, maybe he'd like a few inches in height from me in return. Smiling to myself, I made a mental note to mention this when next I saw him.

Wrapping a scarf around my neck, I walked out the front door, stepped through the gate, and turned left into the lane, in the opposite direction of the village. Water from the previous night's rain was running down the little drainage ditches on both sides of the road. After a few minutes' brisk walking, I came to a T-junction. The lane to the right descended to the road where the bus had dropped me on my arrival. In the distance I could see that it led to a rocky beach. The lane to the left wound upwards towards bleak hills. Because my natural inclination was to go downhill to the beach, rather than uphill into what looked like far less inviting territory, I turned left.

I wanted to experience doing what I wouldn't usually do. In order to be more awake, I intended to break all the conscious and unconscious patterns of behavior that I had developed. Comforting patterns—such as eating, sleeping, and speaking when I wanted—could, I realized, dull my consciousness. Changing my ordinary rote rituals might lead to some interesting experiences. Would I become angry or depressed? Would I have exciting new insights or heightened awareness? Also, I wanted to develop my will power and assert more control over my body. If I had a past life in Greece, it would have been as an Athenian who believed in the beauty and pleasures of life, rather than as a Spartan striving for self-discipline and leading a life of strict self-denial. So today I was taking the opportunity to visit Sparta.

These were my thoughts while walking slowly uphill, and I'd already been rewarded with an insight. I became aware that I expected a reward from self-deprivation. Without being consciously aware of it, my mind had inserted a goal into my walk. I reminded myself to let go of any objective and instead focused on the beauty around me.

Magic has an almost tangible presence in rural Ireland and it can be felt by most sensitive people. The breezes caress and sing to you, and I could feel my aura cleansed and my spirit uplifted. My feet tread lighter on the path as I ascended higher and higher. Rounding a bend, I caught sight of a small cemetery down a path to the left. Aware that all significant roads seemed to be leading left today (the direction of demanifestation and of unmaking what we have made), I headed off in that direction.

As I approached the cemetery, I realized it was very overgrown. Surrounded by field stones piled waist-high, it housed about fifty tombstones. Straight ahead was an iron gate. It creaked loudly on rusty hinges as I pushed it open.

Cemeteries have never been favorite places of mine. My former partner Bill had more than a passing interest in them. In our time together we had visited cemeteries all over the world—from Mexico, where the coffins are stacked in layers above the ground, to cremation sites in Bali.

I don't like cemeteries because I can feel the spirits of the deceased tugging at me. Despite erecting my shield against them, I'm still aware of their presence. It's not that I object to speaking with dead people, or what metaphysicians call "disincarnate entities," but I am choosy about who I speak to, just as I'm choosy about my friends. It's not uncommon for me to speak with my father or others I've known who have passed over, and sometimes I'm given messages from the dead for the living. But I've found that it's the least desirable spirits that hang about cemeteries trying to cling to the material world.

Mentally shielding myself, I approached the tombstones with both caution and respect. Although overgrown, the cemetery appeared to still be used. Flowers had been planted on some of the graves, and faded plastic ones stuck into the ground on others. I walked from plot to plot, noting the dates and names on the stones. Many of them had died very young, over a hundred years ago, and I assumed that their deaths had occurred during the potato famine.

the cemetery

cliffs and sea

Compelled to continue my "aimless" walk, I left, closing the gate behind me again. Immediately I felt a sense of relief and realized that the spirits could not move outside the iron and stone barrier.

To the left of the cemetery was a deeply rutted path that ascended steeply up the hill. Dodging the potholes and brambles, I climbed quickly to the summit where to my surprise I encountered the remains of a deserted village. There were no structures standing, only the bases of what were once small stone houses. Obviously people had not lived there for a very long time, and I wondered if the former inhabitants were the people buried in the cemetery below.

A rolling brown plateau stretched before me. Mounds of peat were drying in the sun, and dark slashes in the earth showed where the sods had been removed. It felt very much like the cemetery I'd just left. At first I thought the plateau deserted, but then I noticed a family of four in the distance, stacking their peat. They hadn't seen me and I was torn between remaining silent or asking them some questions. I decided upon the latter and walked towards them. They noticed me but kept working, and I wondered if I was intruding.

The two children were about four and five years of age. With small buckets and spades, they were building castles in the peat, as if playing with sand on the beach. Their parents were re-stacking their peat so that the wet side would dry. They wore wellies, blue jeans, and heavy Irish wool sweaters.

"Hello," I said, when I was within earshot.

They stopped what they were doing and silently watched me approach. They seemed neither eager nor reluctant to engage in conversation and I decided that a few questions would be well enough received.

"I'm a stranger to Ireland," I said, as if they couldn't tell at a glance, "and I was wondering who was going to use all this peat?"

It seemed to be the man's duty to respond. "Each family in the village owns a piece of the hill and they cut their own turf," he said, leaning on what looked like a special turf-cutting shovel.

I looked around for boundary markers, or some indication of where one plot ended and another began, but couldn't see any. Interpreting my perplexed look, he said with pride, "Each plot has been handed down from generation to generation."

I understood then that no markers were needed; from the time they were children, individuals would come to cut their family's turf and no one would infringe on their neighbors. This was a communal property for the village.

"When is it cut?" I inquired, wanting to understand the entire cycle.

"We cut it in the spring and stack it to dry so that the air can get at it. Then as soon as it's dry, hopefully before too much rain," he laughed, looking at the grey clouds overhead, "we take it down and use it the same year. Most of us still use turf, even if we have central heatin'."

I remembered the sweet smell that had emanated from my burning hearth and could easily see why the Irish would be reluctant to give up peat. I thanked the couple for the information and continued strolling along the peat bog until I could see the village in the distance. At that point I realized that I'd walked three-quarters of a circle and was, even now, on the hill behind my cottage. I couldn't see my cottage but I could make out the lane and Mrs. O'Toole's farm. There was a well-worn path down the hill so I started down the other side towards home. By the time I reached my cottage, the evening was closing in. I was greeted by a warm peat fire burning in the hearth. Mrs. O'Toole had already been and gone. I made myself dinner, sat by the fire musing over the day, and retired early to bed.

CHAPTER SIX

Market Day

T**HE NEXT MORNING** I **AWOKE SLOWLY**, not wanting any more unpleasant surprises. Eyes half-closed, I peered cautiously over the edge of my blankets and was delighted to find that I was alone. I sat up, propped up my pillows behind my back, and pulled on my sweater over my flannel nightie.

What a luxury. This was the first time that I'd had an opportunity to contemplate my morning. Time was passing and one month would soon be gone with me no further along towards enlightenment if I didn't do some meditating. Today, at last, I could meditate in peace, then eat breakfast, meditate a little more, and then go for a walk in the afternoon. My day planned, I closed my eyes and began to focus on my breath. I was just entering a peaceful state when suddenly I was brought back to the surface by a loud knock at the front door. Throwing back the covers, I stepped onto the freezing cold floor, quickly pulled on some socks, and raced for the door.

I opened it a crack, thinking that greeting people in my nightie might not be acceptable in Ireland. A young woman with short straight brown hair smiled back at me.

"Hello," she said, "I'm Maureen, Mrs. O'Toole's daughter. We're going to the next town for the market and wondered if you'd like to come?"

She didn't look a bit like Mrs. O'Toole. My height, probably mid-twenties, with boyish bobbed hair, Maureen had none of the

36

eccentricities of her mother. With her average-small-town-girl look, she would have fit into any North American suburb. Mrs. O'Toole and Maureen were wonderful examples of the differences between the old and modern Ireland.

I quickly considered her offer and accepted. Meditation would still be there tomorrow and this was another chance to practice living in the moment.

"Thank you for inviting me—I'd love to go," I answered. "When are you leaving?"

"In half an hour. We'll pick you up then," she replied, heading briskly towards the gate.

I shut the door, quickly dressed, and made some tea and toast. I made an extra portion for my leprechaun friend and left it on the table. He was nowhere to be seen. Punctually, a half-hour later, a car pulled up in front of the gate. Opening the door, I was greeted by a slender young girl about seven years old. She wore a summer frock with a sweater that didn't look warm enough to me, and knee-high socks completed by city shoes. Her shoulder-length hair was pulled back at the sides by two barrettes.

"I'm Shannon," she said, obviously pleased to have the responsibility of collecting the "American." "We're ready to go now."

I followed her down the path towards the waiting car. The back door swung open and we both got in beside an even younger child.

"I'm Tanis. Who are you?" I said. She was about five, rounder than Shannon, with her mother's boyish brown bob.

"I'm Bridget," she replied, her toothless grin reminding me of her grandmother.

Maureen sat in the passenger seat in the front beside a sturdily-built, good-looking man who eyed me through the rear view mirror. "I'm Brendan," he said smiling. "How are ya settlin' in to the cottage?"

His mildly mischievous tone revealed his surprise at a foreigner choosing to live in such primitive conditions. Most of the younger generation of rural Irish would gladly exchange such cottages for a modern house, and it was difficult for Brendan and Maureen to understand why I'd chosen such a primitive place.

"The cottage is fine," I responded. "I like the quiet."

"Don't you find it damp?" Brendan pressed.

"Yes, it's cold all right. I'm glad your Mom has been helping with the fire. I still haven't mastered it," I said, grinning.

Brendan, his initial curiosity satisfied, put the car in gear and set off rapidly down the lane. Hedges became a blur and, grabbing the door handle, I realized that if we met another car we'd never get by. This was strictly a one-car lane. In Canada, that knowledge would probably have made us drive slower, with more caution. In Ireland, the tendency seemed to be to drive faster and hope that you never meet another car. I was relieved when he spun onto the main road and I could relax back into my seat.

Speeding past hills on the left and sea on the right put me in a reflective mood. It had only been three days since my arrival but it seemed much longer. I was questioning whether I had done the right thing by coming along and mentally drew up a list of things that I might need, in order to justify the trip.

The houses became more closely packed and in a few minutes we were on the main street of a town. Brendan swerved into a parking place, turned off the ignition, and opened the door. We all got out. Without a word he proceeded alone down the street. Maureen and the kids showed no intention of following him, so I fell in with them.

I was amazed that Maureen and Brendan didn't make any kind of arrangement before going off in opposite directions. All seemed to be understood between them. This reminded me of the almost telepathic connection between the couple stacking peat the previous day. Perhaps Maureen and Brendan had taken this journey so many times before that they knew, without asking, what the other was going to do.

While I was musing, Maureen, clutching each child by the hand, started across the street towards a series of market stalls. On the tables were piles of new and used merchandise. Many of the stalls were unattended, as their owners were chatting with their neighbors, an activity that seemed to appeal to them more than selling their goods. The girls pulled Maureen towards a table festooned with barrettes, ribbons, and colored bows. She went willingly while they picked over the selection.

market day

I noticed that many of the locals were wearing Aran sweaters, and they looked warm and well worn. Approaching Maureen, I asked her where I could buy one.

"You'll not get one in the market. You'll have to go to a department store," she replied. Giving it some thought, she came up with the answer. "Murphy's down the road should have jumpers," she said, pointing me in the right direction.

I started off in the direction she'd indicated and soon arrived at an old wooden storefront, with Murphy's written in gold and black letters above the window. I opened the door and walked in, adjusting to the yellow light. They'd not yet heard of fluorescent lighting, thank goodness. An old cash register sat on a counter in the middle of the store, and behind it stood a young woman smiling in my direction. I have Irish ancestry and look Irish outside of Ireland, what with my red hair, sparkling eyes, and what my friends call "a contagious grin," but I knew that she and everyone else could tell that I was an outsider. What was it that didn't fit? I wondered, not for the first time. The young woman came out from behind the counter and said in a lovely lilting voice, "Can I help you, miss?"

"Yes, please, I'm looking for an Aran sweater."

"Hand-knit?" she inquired.

"Yes," I replied, wondering how much more this would cost than a "Made in Korea" version.

She motioned me to the far side of the store where, lined up on several wooden shelves, were Aran sweaters of all sizes and descriptions

Looking at my body to size me up, she pulled a sweater down from the second shelf and handed it to me. "I think this one should fit you," she said encouragingly.

I pulled it on over my head and it fit like a glove. The arms were just the right length and it even hugged me a bit around the waist. "Do you think it's too small?" I asked, already feeling the tremendous warmth of the wool.

"No, it's perfect for you if you take off your other sweater," she volunteered.

"I don't want to be cold," I said, remembering the strong winds on the hillsides.

"You won't be with that," she said, smiling and pointing to the sweater. "It's very warm and water resistant. Even if it gets wet, it'll stay warm."

Convinced, I asked the price.

"Fifty-five pounds," she responded. I must have looked shocked, as she added hurriedly, "Each one is totally unique."

She pulled more sweaters from the shelves and showed me the different patterns. The various cable stitches were, she explained, derived from fishermen's knots and all had names.

"I'll take it," I exclaimed, reaching into my wallet for the money. She rang up my purchase and handed me the sweater, assuring me that I wouldn't be sorry. My mission completed, I started to think longingly of my quiet cottage. Back on the busy street I quickly walked to the market stalls and arrived in time to see Maureen paying for ribbons. The girls ran towards me, eager to show off their new finery. I exclaimed how beautiful they both were and, happy, they took my hand and walked me back to their mother.

Brendan returned just as Maureen was finishing. After browsing briefly at several other stalls, we walked to a small cafe for lunch and ate a meal of fish and chips, the staple fare in this small country town. After washing down the greasy food with hot milky tea, we headed back to the car. I had barely experienced the town, yet it felt good to be going home.

CHAPTER SEVEN

Guidelines for Manifesting

RRIVING AT THE COTTAGE, I discovered the leprechaun seated on the couch, dressed in an Aran sweater identical to the one I had just bought.

"So did you have a good day?" he greeted me, swinging his arms over the back of the couch in a studied human male gesture.

I started to laugh at his relaxed fireside manner and sat down beside him.

"I thought we could talk about manifesting today," he said, eager to forgo the pleasantries. "Now humans don't think they're very good at manifesting. They believe that they have to work hard to get enough food to eat, a place to live, and clothes to wear."

With these last words, he pulled his sweater down over his ample belly, indicating the obvious ease with which he could easily manifest the same sweater that I had to journey to a neighboring town to first find and then buy.

"Now, it is true that you're living in a denser realm and that it is more difficult to manifest in your world. But what humans don't realize is that all their thoughts about what they want, create a reality in other dimensions. These thoughts could easily be brought into your dimension if you weren't so busy canceling them out."

"How do we do that?" I inquired, eager to correct this behavior.

"Humans send two conflicting messages to the universe. One is that I would like such and such. The other is that I don't think I can have it because I don't have enough money or education, or because Sean and Moiré have it. Because humans transmit these contradictory messages, they don't get what they want.

He looked at me smugly and continued, "Elementals don't have this problem."

"I can see that," I responded, gazing pointedly at his sweater and waiting for him to share his secret.

"We think about what we would like and extend our senses to see it and feel it, and then it appears. It works because elementals believe that it will work. The older or stronger elementals become, the better able they are to manifest what they want because they have more energy to put into it."

The leprechaun paused, withdrew his arm from the back of the sofa, and scratched his chin thoughtfully.

"We use up energy in order to manifest," he said. "It would take a lot of energy if we wanted to manifest a cottage." His gaze circled the room to emphasize the significance of such a feat.

"Now, there aren't many of us who could do that," he added hastily, so as not to misinform me.

"That's a nice sweater you're wearing," I said, encouraging him to return to the basics of manifestation. "Does it protect you and keep you warm as mine does?"

"Yes and no," he replied and paused poignantly. "Your realm has more substance, density, and in some cases nourishment for elementals. We like to eat from your realm to increase our density and our energy so that we can manifest more. This is why we are drawn to humans and human things.

"When humans look at a tomato they see it only in one dimension," he continued. "When elementals grow a tomato they beautify it in other dimensions and that beauty seeps through into your dimension and gives it sparkle and zest."

For some moments now, my friend had been gazing at the hearth as he spoke. I had been so intent on his words that I had not been following his gaze. A flash of red caught my eye, and I turned to find a fire blazing in the hearth. I blinked and it instantly disappeared again. The fire was blazing only in his reality while mine held a cold hearth. Opening my senses, I attempted to feel the heat and smell the peat from his fire. Nothing happened.

Following my thoughts, the leprechaun turned to me and said, "Humans have many stories about visiting the faery kingdom where there is beautiful music, clothing, and food; but when they try to eat the food, there is no taste or substance. Because of this, humans accuse us of fraud and trickery. I put it to you this way: is this cottage in which we're living fraud and trickery?"

"If you mean is it solid and can I touch it, I'd say yes," I responded.

"So to you this cottage looks solid?" he queried and, not waiting for an answer, walked to the hearth and proceeded to pass his arm through the stone wall.

"Then, how do you explain this?" he challenged, winking.

"You might be able to do that, but I can't," I responded.

"That's not true; you can do this as well. It's just that you don't believe you can, and that's the difference," he proposed, removing his arm from inside the mantel and returning to the couch.

Taking a deep breath, his philosopher's pose intact, he continued, "Your scientists have recently discovered that you and I and all these things," he gestured to include the couch, walls, and mantel, "aren't solid. There's more space in all of us than water or anything else. Both humans and elementals call this space ether and this ether is mostly what we're composed of. Where humans and elementals differ is that we elementals have a better understanding and working knowledge of ether. This is why we can travel in time and space and manifest what we want so easily."

Looking back at the fire, he explained, "You could light a fire in your reality, as I do in mine. All you have to do is to concentrate and to believe that it's possible. There are wise people in India who are manifesting food all the time. Humans flock to them thinking that they are very special teachers. Some of them are old souls but, regardless, it works because they've discovered that these things are possible."

Shifting his weight, he continued, "There are also psychic surgeons in the Philippines who can pass their hands into a person's body and pull out illnesses. It's all founded on the same belief."

Amazed at his immense knowledge of humans around the world, I wondered, not for the first time, if he were picking up this knowledge from me. I was familiar with both examples he had referred to.

Catching my thought, he grinned at me and explained, "I can read this knowledge from your memory, but also I travel to see these people and things for myself."

He returned his gaze to the fire and sat in silence, waiting. I felt a space open in me and expand outward to the fire. Memories bubbled to the surface—memories of instructions I had been given by my spiritual guides, masters on the inner plane, over the past few years. On several occasions they had pointed out to me that I was a much better receiver than sender of information in the etheric realms. I had been told to practice concentration in order to improve my ability to manifest what I wanted. One of the exercises they asked me to do was to sit in front of a hearth filled with kindling, paper, and wood, and to imagine lighting it without a match. I had attempted this exercise several times without success. This, as the leprechaun pointed out, was due to my deep-rooted belief that what I was attempting to do was impossible. I believed that other humans could do this, but I had no direct personal experience on which to ground the belief that this was possible for me.

"Can you put out a fire as easily as you start one?" I asked.

"Of course," he laughed incredulously. "The principles are the same both for manifesting and demanifesting. One moment I concentrate on wanting a fire and see the image as I want it and it happens. The next moment I think and see a cold hearth and it happens."

"You mentioned earlier that humans think the jewels and food in your realm are trickery. Are they as real for you in your reality as these things are real for me in mine?" I inquired.

"That's not the best way of asking the question," he corrected me, unlocking his hands from behind his head and placing them over his belly.

"It would be better to ask if there is a life force in what we manifest, and to this question the answer is yes. Our food can be eaten and our jewels are real to us. However, this life force in our world is not as great as the life force in your reality. Therefore, whereas it can sustain us, it wouldn't be able to sustain most humans. Elementals can live off the essence of human food but most humans couldn't live off the essence of our food."

He paused, looked at me knowingly, and continued, "I say 'most humans' because there are notable exceptions. We sometimes welcome humans into our world for long periods of time—occasionally for their entire lives—but that's another story."

With these words he stood up and made ready to leave. I was in the process of wondering why he couldn't stay longer, when he replied, "I've got things to do and our friend Mrs. O'Toole will be here to light the fire before long."

With those words he slowly faded. The Aran sweater was the last thing to disappear. I sat there for a few minutes, then heard the gate squeak open, followed by a knock on the door. Mrs. O'Toole had arrived.

CHAPTER EIGHT

Time Out of Time

T HE NEXT MORNING I had finished breakfast and was sitting on the couch sipping my second cup of tea. The tea I'd set out for my leprechaun friend sat on the floor getting cold. During the last half hour I had felt a mounting sense of anxiety. The summer was passing and I felt no closer to enlightenment than when I had arrived. Was I spending my time wisely or wasting it? I planned to develop a regime for the rest of my stay—meditation, fasting, silence. The prospect did not fill me with joy, but it seemed like a necessary means to an end. Yet I found myself unwilling to commit to action and continued to fill in the details of the plan— various meditation techniques and fasting methods. Perhaps a little variety might help to motivate me.

Still not quite ready to begin my day, I gazed lazily around the room. My eyes came to an abrupt halt at the bedroom doorway where three seemingly disembodied heads had appeared. Like living wall trophies, my leprechaun friend and his two children were stacked on top of each other, grinning from ear to ear. I burst into laughter and immediately felt my anxiety dissolve.

My friend, eyes still twinkling, spoke, "Well, that's better. You were taking this enlightenment thing too seriously." All three faces withdrew from the door frame and my friend reappeared, dressed in his Aran sweater, his short legs dangling over the edge of the couch.

47

Looking down at the Aran knit, he asked, "What do you think of this?" and green shamrocks suddenly appeared all over his copious belly.

"I think it's a bit gaudy," I replied honestly.

"Then what about this?" he asked, changing the pattern to one big shamrock across his chest. It was tamer, but still gaudy for my taste.

"I prefer the pattern of the knit. It's quite intricate enough," I commented.

He huffed disagreement but the shamrock dissolved and reappeared as a three-inch brooch pinned to his left chest, where humans commonly wear pins.

"Bor-ring!" he exclaimed, mocking human slang, and then started chortling in glee at his own cleverness.

"Well," he said, more sober, "isn't this more fun than meditating?"

"Maybe it is," I allowed, "but I'm concerned that I may be wasting my time by not staying focused on my real purpose for being here."

"Isn't that just like a human," he exclaimed, "thinking your purpose has to be solemn and serious, rather than fun."

"I'll concede that fun, joy, and beauty are important," I admitted, "but don't we also need to focus on where we're going, rather than just on where we are?"

"Oh, absolutely!" my friend agreed. "That's what humans are so good at and that's one of the things you are teaching me this summer. Humans can teach elementals focus and direction. You see, we perceive time differently."

I sat quietly, sipping my tea and waiting for him to continue.

"Humans think that there's a beginning, a middle, and an end," he said, resuming his scholarly pose "a past, present, and future. You see these moments of time in little boxes. This is very different from the kind of relationship that elementals have with time. For us, there are various options from which we choose, and we don't fix on one possibility. Humans think there is only one past and that there will be only one future, which cannot be known in advance. But I can look at you and know all the options you've experienced—not just in this life but in past lives also. And not just past lives on this one track that you believe you're on, but on all the optional tracks you've experienced."

"Seth's book *Oversoul Seven,*" I interjected, eager to show that I had heard of these thoughts before, "talks about how a soul can be in various personalities and different time periods simultaneously. Are you referring to this?"

"To be sure," he replied, "and I know that you embrace the theory, but you can't remember an experience of this. That's the difference between us."

"I can remember many of my past lives," I responded.

"Aye, but they are only on one track. Would you like to experience a life on another track."

"Of course!" I exclaimed, eager to proceed.

He smiled at my enthusiasm and asked, "Did you know that you had a life living with elementals?"

"No, I didn't. How did that occur?" I said, impatiently.

"We spoke before of elementals who incorporated into human evolution. Well, some humans have entered elemental evolution to learn more about us and to help us with the qualities we need to learn from humans. They are hybrids and you are one of these."

It was amazing to hear something about myself of which I had no knowledge. Still, his words felt right in my body, even though I lacked a conscious memory.

"Oh, you have the memory, you just haven't remembered it yet," laughed my friend. "In your time sense, this occurred hundreds of years ago but elementals can still read this on you and know that you are friendly to us."

"Could I remember that life?" I asked, my curiosity piqued.

"Of course," he responded intently, gesturing for me to close my eyes.

As my eyes closed, I immediately saw myself dressed in a long brown woolen skirt that grazed the ground. I was walking along a path covered in autumn leaves. All around me was a magical forest. I felt the life force and identity of each tree and knew that I could visualize any season that I wanted and it would appear. Spring was wanting to emerge, but I resisted the urge to encourage it. Opening my ears as I walked, I heard the birds and animals talking to each other. I understood all their chirps and yelps and thoughts.

My hair was longer than I wear it now, and I was older—about forty. Even though I was surrounded by beauty, I was filled with sorrow, for I knew that I was leaving. I became aware that someone was watching me and turned to see a tall, elegant, slender man dressed in forest green. He observed my approach and, when I was almost upon him, took off his pointed cap and bowed elaborately before me. His hands were long and delicate and he moved with flawless grace. His eyes were a deep green, slightly slanted, and not human.

"Good morrow, wise one," he greeted me. "Where are you going today?"

"I'm going to my death," I whispered softly.

"And why choose death?" he inquired, sorrow filling his eyes. "Are you not happy amongst us?"

"I have been happy," I replied. "I'll miss the magic of the forest and talking with all its creatures. But something in my soul calls me to leave."

"Oh, a soul call," he replied, sadness moving across his face. "We must obey that."

I blinked and found myself farther down the path and he far behind me. I heard him call after me, "Do not forget us," and his voice echoed through the forest.

Turning my head back in the direction I had been walking, I saw a beautiful light beckon me. I lifted off the ground towards it and when I looked back saw my physical body lying on the path, already being covered by leaves. I turned back towards the light and entered it. I lost consciousness and remembered nothing.

Returning to the present, I opened my eyes to find my leprechaun friend watching me intently.

"Why did he call me 'wise one'?" I asked, "I was only middle-aged."

"If you'd looked around, you would have found that not many elementals take on an old shape. They usually keep their youthful look even if they are old. Only a few," and he pointed his finger at himself, "take on the shape of their real age."

"Also," the leprechaun hesitated, "you gave a lot to elementals in that life. You were respectful of our ways but taught us how humans think and act, so that we could understand them better. At that time elementals had not yet decided to become creators, but the seeds were being sown. Some of us could feel the change in the stream of time that led to you and other humans who would teach us."

When my friend stopped speaking, I saw for the first time deep respect and affection in his eyes. There was no acting, just sincere emotion. I was filled with love for him and for all those I'd known but couldn't quite remember.

Not wishing to break the magic of the moment, I spoke gently. "That man in the forest . . . I felt as if I knew him; did I?"

"Aye, you knew him well. You spent many years in his company," the leprechaun replied succinctly.

I had never known him to be so hesitant to give out information but I pushed a little further. "What is he doing now?" I inquired.

"Do you really want to see that?" my friend exhaled softly, hoping that I'd say no.

"Perhaps not yet," I replied, trusting his judgment.

He cleared his throat and, without warning, launched himself off the couch and into the air, landing squarely on the floor. He reminded me of people being shot out of cannons at the circus. Straightening his sweater, he announced, "I think we need an exercise break."

He then proceeded to run around the couch at lightning speed. He was so quick that you could hardly tell, while looking at one spot, if he was coming or going. The run completed, he got down on the floor and began twisting himself into odd configurations that were half aerobics and half yoga. Once again his speed was at least triple what a human could achieve. It was obvious that he had seen humans doing these things in many different places and had thrown together Californian and Indian techniques in a combination that only he could master. I had images of him teaching his "fitness system" to the gnomes and goblins, and collapsed into gales of laughter.

"So what's wrong with my exercise program?" he demanded, hands on hips and legs akimbo.

"Nothing, nothing," I gasped, attempting to be serious but not succeeding.

Face now red and fuming, he accused, "Then why are you laughing?"

I realized he thought I was mocking him—a big mistake given how seriously he took his mastery of human behaviors. I put on my most apologetic look—sincere, if slightly exaggerated—in a manner resembling his imitations of humans. He looked at me, understood my intent, and broke into rolling guffaws.

Throwing himself back on the couch, he reached over to shake my arm and gasped, with tears running down his cheeks, "You've done it. You've done it."

"What have I done?" I inquired, puzzled.

"Why, you've one-upped me, of course," he laughed.

I then realized that I'd achieved a kind of leprechaun award. I'd outsmarted an elemental at his own game.

This made me wonder about the different standards of acceptable behavior between our two races. "Do you really have exercise breaks like that?" I asked.

Still smiling, he replied, "Well, I've really learned those exercises from humans but I did have a reason for doing them."

"Other than to master everything human, you mean?" I interrupted with a grin.

Shaking his finger at me, my friend responded, "You'd better be careful, you'll turn into an elemental. . . ."

"And you'll turn into a human," I countered, cutting him off.

"You're getting quicker. Good. But would you like to talk about what elementals are learning from humans?" he asked.

"Yes!" I responded, finding it difficult to regain my composure. I half-wondered if he were contaminating me.

Smiling at my insight, the leprechaun confirmed my thought and took it one step further.

"We fertilize each other," he said, gesturing towards me. "If humans associate with elementals, they become more elemental, and vice versa. For a human, you have a very playful, childlike personality, with a mischievous sense of humor. Where do you think you got that?"

Intrigued, I responded, "My mother's family are all like that. I thought I got it from them."

"And so you did, but they're all Irish aren't they? So where do you think they got it from?"

"From leprechauns?" I inquired, knowing this was the deduction he wanted me to make.

"Exactly," my friend nodded, happy that I could follow his "logic."

He continued, "There's another reason why you've got some elemental in your personality. You've had more than one life living and working with us. What you saw earlier was just one of those lives."

"So," I interjected, "if I've been learning joy, mischievous humor, and quickness, what have I been teaching elementals in those lives?"

"Mostly it comes down to responsibility and love," he replied. "But to employ these, we have to have concentration. It's hard for us to hold our concentration for long on any one topic. I've trained myself for decades, but it's not easy for elementals. In human stories about elementals, we are accused of being changeable. Humans say that we fall in love with one person and then leave them because we fall in love with someone else. By human standards there is a lot of truth in this, because we love variety. We like to experience all feelings and every new thing."

He looked over at me and I could read his thought before he spoke. "Aye, even this you got from us. Look at how many careers you have going at the same time. You're a therapist, an 'organizational consultant' as you call it, a spiritual teacher, and now an author, and you've worked already in about twenty jobs and spent years traveling all over the world. That changeability is very elemental."

I agreed with some of what he was saying, but not that I was fickle in love. I was about to defend myself when he continued.

"You are very loyal to your friends and loved ones, but that's for a different reason. That's because you have a very well-developed sense of responsibility and love, and that," he paused, "is human."

Looking somewhat shamefaced, my friend glanced away from me. I had no idea what had caused his shame and was surprised when he added, "In some ways we've harmed you."

He looked up to see the affect of his words. I didn't feel harmed but was curious to know more.

He swung around to face me and said, "Living with elementals has harmed your concentration because you get bored easily, like us."

He seemed to want to get everything out at once and continued, "Not only that, but you're forever discontent with your life. That's because, in your body and unconscious memories, you've known so much magic living with us. The human world is not nearly as appealing to you now."

I could easily forgive the fact that I'd lost my concentration, even though I knew it was a weakness. I had battled with boredom and lack of self-discipline for many years. It was this last point about my ongoing discontent with the "real world" that really touched me.

An image from childhood suddenly flashed before me. I was about eight or nine and still in love with Peter Pan. I desperately wanted to go to Never-never land where I wouldn't have to grow up. At that time, my parents had a hardware store in Toronto and we lived in an apartment above it. One day when they were working downstairs, I saw sunbeams coming through my bedroom skylight, creating rainbows in the dust particles suspended in the air. It looked like the faery dust that Tinkerbell sprinkled on children so they could fly.

I pushed my dresser across the room, placing it beneath the shaft of faery dust. Using a chair, I climbed onto the top of the dresser and stood there, eyes closed, as I waited for the faery dust to work. I felt the warmth of the sun and my spirit soared. Wishing ever so hard that I could fly, I launched myself off the dresser into the air and hit the floor with a wallop. Not dissuaded, I climbed back on top of the dresser and tried again. Crash. I did this over and over again and finally was lying bruised and battered on the floor when the bedroom door opened.

My mother surveyed the room and put two and two together. Annoyed she said, "You'll have to stop jumping; we can hear you downstairs in the store." With that she walked out, closing the door behind her. That was the end of my childhood. I realized at that moment, that no matter how hard I wished and believed in Never-never land, I could never go there. For me, the faery kingdom still existed but there was obviously something wrong with me so that I couldn't go.

My leprechaun friend sat attentively on the couch, watching me relive that memory. "I was in love with the Peter Pan story because that was the gateway back to the faery kingdom, right?" I asked quietly.

"That's right. In some other lives you came to us as a human child and wanted to do so again. However, that was not appropriate at this time in our evolution—neither for you personally, nor for humans as a race.

"The Peter Pan story is important to humans because it reminds them of a magical time when they could come into our world and play without limits and confinement," continued the leprechaun. "This is part of the human racial memory."

"So," I said, returning to his original point, "is there a cure for my discontent with the limitations of what I can do in the human world?"

"Well, part of your cure is to realize that many of these limitations are imaginary. For example, you can see and talk with me and with many beings in other realms. This you already know," he replied.

"True, but other humans don't always believe this," I said, remembering the years of rejection.

"Stop whining," my friend said, raising his voice. "Many elementals regard humans as the enemy who are killing us. Do you think all elementals agree that I should be studying and working with humans?"

"I'm sorry, you're right of course," I replied, chastened. "In any event, what else can I do about the discontent?"

"Enjoy all the gifts we have given you," he answered. "Gifts of laughter, joy, curiosity, and enthusiasm. When you express these gifts, humans are attracted and they open to these qualities in themselves. This is important for our two races to work harmoniously together.

"Also, believe that you can do much more than you have thought possible. You can manifest almost anything you want. This is an awesome power," he commented, "but, to do this, you must improve your powers of concentration, just as we elementals need to do."

"To be honest," I interjected, "I'm afraid to believe that I can manifest almost anything that I want because there's a huge responsibility attached. I'm not a perfect person, so what if I manifest something that is not helpful to myself or to others?"

"Fear, added to conscience, results in never taking chances in your life. You dream only the small dream," my friend said, throwing up his hands in mock exasperation.

"What you need to realize is that you are already loving and responsible enough. You're teaching us that, remember? Now you need to practice concentration."

"Okay, I'm convinced," I retorted. "Tell me how elementals concentrate."

"Elementals can work together to hold thoughts and to increase the power of each other's manifestation," the leprechaun answered. "In the past we did this on large-scale projects, such as during wars and the building of cities. Also, sometimes we took over holding a manifestation for someone else so that he could have a break."

Suddenly his face became very sad. He continued, "Our world has become very different in the last several hundred years. With the invasion of humans, we have had to abandon cities and large parts of our world. We could no longer hold our manifestations with all the human thoughts crowding in. So we have lost much beauty and joy in our realm."

As he spoke, I could sense the weight of responsibility that he carried for his people, and his desire to create a new way of life for them.

"I'm surprised that as an elemental you can feel such a deep sense of responsibility for your race." I said.

Still despondent, he replied, "You're right, it's not what elementals are like normally. But it's what the group, to which I belong, is developing."

"You're doing very well. You almost feel human but it's a pity that it makes you so sad," I said, only too familiar with the weight of responsibility.

"We both lose something when we learn from each other's evolution," the leprechaun replied. "Humans are often sad because, weighed down with duty and responsibility, their joy leaves. We elementals are trying to find ways to be uplifted by our responsibility so that we won't lose the essence of what we are."

"I agree," I said. "There's no reason why humans can't be both joyful and responsible at the same time."

"And I'm gaining something else from humans," he continued on a more cheerful note. "I am learning to love. Now you're way ahead of us on that. Your love, not only for your friends and your family but even for strangers, is admirable. Through denying ourselves immediate pleasure, we have been learning love. Not all elementals manage this of course, but now we have the seeds in our evolution. The more we associate with spiritual humans, the more we learn love."

I had a sudden insight. "If I love you," I asked, "can you feed on it as you feed on toast and tea?"

He smiled, his old cheekiness resurfacing.

"Absolutely!" he replied. "The more humans love us, the more we can feel this emotion and replicate it in ourselves. You become what you eat, as you know."

"Even if elementals are fickle in loving each other, don't they still love the Earth?" I wondered aloud.

"This is instinctive in us," the leprechaun replied. "Elementals want to create beauty and joy and because of this we make the Earth more beautiful. Within our group we are focusing our attentions on what's most needed both by our people and by others on Earth. This is a newly-learned behavior. As we do this, we develop our free will, and this is the purpose of the choice that we've made."

In listening to him, I suddenly realized that this was similar to the Bodhisattva vow taken by Buddhists, which is to reincarnate until "all" sentient beings are enlightened and become conscious creators.

"It is," said he. "Remember when we first met, I told you that you and I were taking the same test and initiation this summer."

An important shift had occurred during our conversation. Before this, we had been focusing more on the differences between elementals and humans. Now I could see in how many ways we were similar.

"That's definitely enough for today," he said, yawning and stretching. "You need to get out and clear your head and then practice meditation this afternoon."

"Did I hear that right?" I joked with him. "You want me to meditate? I thought you were saving me from it."

"Meditation is good for building up discipline," he replied, getting to his feet. "It's just that we don't want you to do too much of it. Aren't we both interested in the middle way of balance?"

With that he disappeared and in the faint echo that followed I heard, "See you tomorrow."

CHAPTER NINE

An Average Day

 OMORROW" FOR LEPRECHAUNS must not have had the same meaning that it had for humans, as it was many tomorrows before our next chat. Days passed through a filter of rain and grey mist and I developed my own routine. I woke at around eight in the morning, pulled on my wool sweater over my nightie, and sat up in bed to meditate. It was so damp I could feel the moisture clinging to my skin and infiltrating my clothes. There seemed to be no difference in temperature between outside and inside the cottage. In fact, with the clammy stone walls, it's possible that inside was even colder.

By about nine o'clock my empty stomach finally provided enough incentive to leave my cozy bed for a cup of tea. Waiting for the water to boil, I filled up three bottles with hot water from the tap and placed them under a blanket on the couch to warm up my seat. My mornings were spent editing the manuscript of *Decoding Destiny,* the book I'd been writing that year. When that was finished, I turned my attention to Dante's *Inferno* and contemplated my own journey through the stages of hell, which Dante described so well.

Sometime around noon, after munching a few slices of toasted Irish soda bread, I put on my calf-length, "water-resistant" raincoat and Queen Elizabeth kerchief and headed down the lane to the sea.

seaside walk

During this walking meditation, I released what was no longer positive and constructive in my life and welcomed what was. In order to avoid meeting anyone so that I could remain silent, I circled the village. Day after day I walked in the rain for hours through country lanes and along the beach where booming surf loosened the knots that held me together, untying old fears, angers, and hurts. Each drop of water dissolved the old me and fertilized the new ground for planting. Occasionally my leprechaun friend came on these walks but mostly he left me alone to contemplate in silence.

Some days found me in a trough of despair, my tears mingling with the rain drops. With an aching heart I put one foot in front of the other. On other days the sun emerged for a brief time, catapulting me into joy and love of life. The yellow and purple irises, white daisies, and purple clover in the fields glistened as the sun struck their wet petals, and rainbows arched over the sea promising a wonderful morrow.

If only those moments could have lasted. Like Wordsworth in his "Intimations of Immortality," I found myself straining back to my innocent childhood, remembering the joys of being fully awake to nature. Then my blood sang again, joy was rekindled in my veins, and I celebrated my good fortune in being right where I was at that very moment.

Whatever thought I thought, whatever feeling I felt, I allowed myself to experience fully during those walks. It was a good internal spring-cleaning. A few times a week I entered the village to buy food. The grocer's was an obstacle course of curious eyes but other than being asked regularly, "How are ya gettin' on at the Davidson's cottage?" I was left alone. Always I was careful to arrive home in time for Mrs. O'Toole's daily visit and the turf-lighting ritual.

Mrs. O'Toole never asked how I was spending my days or nights. One day I received a package of chocolate from home and I offered her some with a cup of tea.

"That would be nice," she replied, politely taking a piece and sitting in silence waiting for the smoldering turf to catch.

After many minutes had elapsed and the blazing turf was filling the room with its own musky, homey smell, I offered her another piece of chocolate. Smiling her toothless grin and eyes twinkling like a child receiving a rare treat, she helped herself to a large chunk.

My leprechaun friend occasionally visited when Mrs. O'Toole was there and the day of the chocolate was one of them. As there was no room on the couch, he perched himself on one of the dining-room chairs and, with notebook and pen on his lap, took copious notes.

After Mrs. O'Toole had left I turned to him and asked, "What did you discover?"

"Fascinating. Fascinating," he drawled in his best British professor voice, with a pince-nez perched on the tip of his bulbous nose.

Tapping the pencil on his notebook to reinforce his points, he continued, "When you and your sweet-toothed friend sit together, the energy around both of you changes. Normally, your energy is more like a bubbling brook, peeping and bouncing around rocks, and her energy is like the ocean surging in and out. When you are together you become more like an ocean, and she becomes more like a bubbling brook. She calms you, and you rekindle her mischievousness.

"You know she's got some of our blood?" he said, peering over the top of his spectacles.

"What kind of elemental is she?" I asked.

the "coos"

"It's a caste you haven't had much contact with," he replied, pushing his spectacles back on his nose and extending his arm with a flourish. "She's one of the coo people. These are the ones who work with all manner of animals. They know all about what animals think and feel.

"She extends her energy through you, just as she does with animals, and affects you like a cat or dog would. When she is with coos or her sheep dog, she doesn't have to talk. They understand each other. This is the way it is with you and her. You don't talk much but you settle into each other's aura and affect each other."

I interrupted to inquire, "Is this what you observed while watching us earlier?"

"Aye," he replied, "I've seen her with animals and was eager to see if she had the same effect on you."

"I'm curious to see these notes you've been taking," I said, gesturing towards his notebook.

"No, no, no," he retorted, clutching his notebook to his chest. "You wouldn't be interested."

"Actually, I am interested because I had no idea that you could write," I countered, reaching forward for the notebook.

"We have a kind of writing," he hedged, pulling away even further.

Trying to put him at ease, I sat back and continued, "So are you saying that you don't read and write like humans?"

Relaxing, his notebook back in his lap, he replied, "That's correct."

Overwhelmed with curiosity, I smiled my most winning smile and inquired, "Could I please have a look at what you've been recording?"

"You probably won't understand," he cautioned, but I could tell he was weakening.

I suddenly realized that part of his reluctance to show me his notebook had to do with his lack of mastery of the human skills of reading and writing. This was a blow to his pride.

"I'm interested to learn as much about elementals as you know about humans," I said, projecting trust and respect towards him.

My friend sat forward and extended his notebook for me to see. There was nothing but a blank page. Looking up at him, I admitted, "I can't see anything."

"That's because we think something onto the page, and the page tells us the images that have been thought onto it," he answered, gesturing for me to try.

Looking again, I could see Mrs. O'Toole and me recorded exactly the way things had happened and moving like a holograph. It was a three-dimensional image, quite superior to our two-

stacking the hay

dimensional television images. To my human eyes it was still vague and filmy, but I could see it. I looked at my friend and smiled at my success.

"Not many of us elementals do this—mainly just the scholars and healers," he said, smiling back. "Elementals read human books the same way that we communicate with you—that is, telepathically. That way, we can read French and German. Novels are easier to read because we can see the images that the writer used when he or she wrote. It's more difficult to read science books unless people thought in images when they wrote.

"There's not a great need to write in our world. Elementals can think and create whatever they wish, so why would we want to create a memory of it. You see, space and time have no barriers for us so we can go to the past or the future and create what was and what will be. Humans can't travel in space and time so they need to record things. Our scholars have learned to write and read because humans need this."

I now understood that the way elementals read, write, and speak had to do with the mind rather than with the movement of the eyes, hands, and mouth. I realized that humans could manifest these qualities as well, if they practiced.

"You're right," the leprechaun said, "and you will do this in the future. Humans had these abilities in Atlantis but they have forgotten them. The strength of the mind and the strength of the will are the keys to manifesting for all beings. Humans exist in a denser reality than elementals, so this is why you must work physically as well as with the mind to manifest what you would like. On the whole, human minds are stronger than the minds of elementals because, to manifest anything, humans need to overcome the resistance of their denser reality, using their will power. This kind of resistance strengthens humans. Unfortunately there are many humans who are weak-minded and follow others' thoughts and feelings. They don't learn to exert their own mind because it requires more effort.

"There are many more humans than elementals who are not manifesting their potential. Humans are too passive. But the humans who do manifest are a great deal stronger than almost all elementals, if they only knew it."

Following my friend's train of thought, I began to wonder if elementals used their bodies to create products or if it was all in their minds. "Do the shoemakers actually make shoes physically or do they just create an illusion that they are making shoes?" I asked.

"Our craft guilds," he began, "make things physically for our reality. They work with heavier elements than most other elementals. The craftsmen in these guilds are the closest to humans in their ability to work with the physical reality. In your folklore, as you call it, there are stories about humans being given objects of superb craftsmanship, made by elementals. Our craftsmen make beautiful jewelry from gems, gold, silver, and copper. Some craft guilds make weapons; others make beautiful books with wonderful covers and borders for the images.

"Our healers have strong minds and ask flowers and trees to provide their life essence for their potions so that they can heal other beings. By just looking at a tree, a human, or an animal, these healers know what essence that being needs and can ask for that essence from some other place in nature. The nature kingdom gives its essence to our healers because all living things work with the divine plan of the creator when they do this."

As he spoke, I was reminded of the human practices of homeopathy and aromatherapy, and said, "We have humans who heal in a similar way."

"To be sure there are," he nodded in agreement.

"Are humans working with the elemental kingdom when they practice these healing techniques?"

"Yes indeed," he continued. "Humans also do this when they grow food. When your farmers put a seed in the ground, they imagine it growing into a strong plant that gives good fruit. If they keep that image in mind, they usually get what they've imagined, if the seed was strong, the earth was good, and there was the right amount of sun. The farmer still needs to work with nature to plant the seed. You can't just plant the seed anywhere. Humans could create wonderful food, beautiful gardens, and healthy trees if they listened to what nature wanted, as well as having the ability to visualize it happening.

CHAPTER TEN

A Date
for the Evening

 WAS BORED and couldn't face another meal on my own at home. The simple dishes I prepared on the two-burner hot plate did little to nourish my soul; I was salivating at the thought of a homemade pastry—any pastry. During my walks I'd discovered a little inn on the seashore just outside the village and had been saving it for just such an emergency. So, afternoon waning, I took my only skirt and blouse from the wardrobe and laid them carefully on the bed.

Savoring the novel experience of a night out, I decided that the luxury of a hot bath was in order. I trotted to the bathroom and, carefully removing the resident spider from the bathtub, put him in the corner.

"Stay," I commanded and he obliged me for the instant. Spiders are like cats. They live alongside humans but refuse to give up their independence.

The large old-fashioned taps squeaked noisily and in less than a minute steam was filling the room. Lacking bubble bath, I squirted some shampoo under the running water and frothed it up. Quickly pulling off my clothes to avoid the damp chill air, I slid into the foam.

Delicious. Sighing, I sank lower into the water and closed my eyes for a moment of bliss. Opening them, I saw the leprechaun perched on top of my clothes on the toilet seat. He was watching me quietly. I grabbed the washcloth and slapped it over my breasts.

"How about a little privacy," I said, glaring at him and sliding lower into the water.

"Just pretend I'm a lover or husband and that we're going out on a date," he exclaimed, crossing one leg over the other in an attempt to look nonchalant. It might have been more convincing if his feet had reached the floor.

"A date," I countered. "I thought that I'd have a night out alone for good behavior. Just me and me—not me and you."

"Would you deny me the full experience of one of your most important human rituals?"

"Which is. . . ?" I cut in, before he could finish.

"Dating, of course," he said, offended.

Still holding my washcloth to my chest, I reached forward and turned on more hot water. Relaxing back against the tub, I closed my eyes to consider. He had a way of getting me to see things differently and he was excellent company but . . . did he think we would become lovers?

My eyes flicked open to find him grinning mischievously at me.

"Why don't we just go minute by minute and see what wants to happen," he proffered good humoredly. Trying to get me to relax, he resumed his scholarly pose and asked, "How's the bath?"

Laughing, I said, "Why don't you take off your clothes and come in."

"I suppose I'd get the end with the taps," he said, casting his eyes down in disapproval.

"Of course," I said, "ladies always get the comfy end."

In the blink of an eye he was in up to his chin, with only his head visible above the foam. The taps had disappeared and the tub behind him was a smooth replica of the tub behind me. He leaned back, extended his bare arms up on the rim and, eyes mocking, said, "Why suffer needlessly? In my world, no one needs to lean against the taps."

As he spoke, the taps emerged on the side of the tub, exactly halfway between us. He leaned forward and added some cold water.

"Do all humans like it this hot?" he exclaimed, fanning his beet-red face for emphasis.

"I think women might like it hotter than men," I replied. "But I've never done a survey; that's just based on my personal experience."

His notebook appeared above his head and, with pen in hand, he recorded what I'd said. I closed my eyes again to relax and immediately became aware that my body was stretched out through his area of the bath. Embarrassed I pulled my knees up and opened my eyes.

"What's the problem?" he asked, smirking in his knowing way.

"You know what the problem is. We're both nude in here and I feel uncomfortable not knowing what to expect next," I replied.

"Next has already happened," he said, allowing his arms to slip under the water. "Water conducts our vibrations to each other more than air, so we are already touching and our essences are mingling. It started to happen as soon as I jumped into the water."

Sitting up straight and pulling the washcloth into position, I exclaimed, "Well, you might have asked me if that was okay."

"Well, you did invite me!" he retorted in a mock show of the misunderstood lover.

Laughing at the hilarity of our situation, I shoved some foam in his face. If he wanted to play the dating game, then he might as well get the full treatment. Eyes twinkling wickedly, he flicked his fingers and the wave swept back on me and dragged the washcloth off my breast.

"I surrender, I surrender," I said, laughing. "You've got a date for the evening, but because you're a 'new' date, I can't shave my armpits while you're here, so you'll have to leave."

"Well, let's pretend I'm an 'old' date, 'cos I want to see that," he said.

Shrugging my shoulders, I picked up the razor and stated, "In the interest of your study of humans I will agree." I then proceeded, with as much dignity as I could muster, to soap my underarms. Raising my left arm above my head, I eyed two weeks of growth and attacked it with gusto.

My friend leaned over and surveyed the procedure with awe. "Elemental women don't shave under their arms," he said.

"Do you mean that they don't have hair there?" I asked.

"Well, goblins and gnomes and some others have hair in lots of places but our ladies from the princely caste don't, and that's what you're looking more like now." He blushed as he spoke.

I felt that he was attracted to some of these ladies but that he was excluded from being lovers with them. Listening to my thought, his blush deepened.

"Why can't you be lovers with them?" I probed gently.

"We are a different caste and the castes do not share sexual energies together. It's taboo," he stated.

"Why?" I asked quickly, my curiosity growing.

"As I've mentioned before, we elementals are lighter than you humans and when we first incarnate we have little substance and hardly know who we are. If we were to blend our energies with another caste at that time we might totally forget ourselves and be annihilated. So the beings who control our evolution instruct us not to do so."

"Humans are not that different, only in degree," I asserted. "When we have sexual intercourse with another human we carry their vibrations for a long time. That's why we think about our lovers so much. It's wonderful fun but lovers distract us from other parts of our life. Few humans die of falling in love, but some do become obsessed with it."

"Humans have much stronger egos than elementals, so you are not in danger of losing yourselves as we are," my leprechaun friend observed.

"When the egos of elementals become stronger as they mature, say, to the stage that you are at now," I said, nodding to my friend, "can they exchange sexual energies with members of other castes?"

He squirmed uncomfortably and answered, "It does happen occasionally, but it's frowned upon in our society and those that do so are usually exiled from their castes and isolated on their own."

"I don't understand this. Many humans have lived in your world and been lovers of elementals and there was no taboo for them. How is it different?" I asked.

Somewhat embarrassed, he replied, "Humans are our sexual outlet. You're a combination of many of our castes all rolled together. Some of you are tall and elegant, like our nobles. Others are short and stocky with bowed legs, like our dwarfs. Some even look like me," he said, chuckling at his own joke.

"Also," he continued, "the humans that are drawn into our world learn from us as we learn from them. It's mostly those of the noble caste who take humans as lovers. They have strong egos and this sharing of energies strengthens them further. There is some danger involved but there is a great deal to be gained from sharing sexual energy with humans. It's like having a blood transfusion of your essence with ours. It catalyzes our evolution to become creators on this planet."

Listening to his explanation, I wondered about the possible danger to humans.

"The danger to humans," he said, responding to my thought, "is that they will fall so much in love with the beauty, magic, and joy in our world that they will not want to leave. Elementals— especially the noble caste—find old age repulsive, so when humans start to age, elementals may not want to be around them. They become more and more isolated, and if they returned to the human world, all their friends and family would be dead."

I shivered. The bath water had cooled rapidly. Debating whether to get out or add more hot water, I sat for a few seconds doing nothing. I had lots more questions to ask and yet was becoming increasingly uncomfortable.

In a flash my friend was back on the toilet seat. He was

wrapped in a deep purple towel that kept reflecting different images. "Don't get cold," he said, rising and turning towards the door. "We can continue this conversation on the way to dinner."

Left alone, I pulled the plug and shivered as the icy damp air hit my body. Grabbing my towel, I rubbed vigorously to stay warm and headed towards the bedroom. It was still light outside and it had stopped raining. I pulled on my stockings for the first time in weeks and wriggled into my skirt without too much difficulty; the cumulative effect of buttered soda bread had created a slight bulge around the waistband. Buttoning up the blouse, I felt the familiar chill in my bones and knew the sweater would once again be needed. As it was a special occasion, I put in my contact lenses, added some lipstick and eyeliner, and was ready for "my date."

Too bad he can't pay, was my last thought as I swung my purse over my shoulder and left the bedroom. The leprechaun awaited me at the front door. He was dressed in a black silk jacket with a cape. Seeing me, he removed his top hat and bowed deeply.

"How lovely you look, my lady," he said in a cavalier manner.

"And you too, sir," I returned with a curtsy.

Together we swept out the door and into the lane. Turning right towards the village, I was astonished to see two rows of elementals lined up on either side of the lane watching us. My leprechaun friend hooked his arm through mine, drew himself up to his full height of four feet, and nodding regally from side to side, started forward. Cheers and guffaws erupted from all sides. We were the night's entertainment for the local denizens.

My friend was enjoying the show immensely. I was sure he had slipped a word to them in advance to prepare them for our night out. Following his example, I nodded and smiled, trying to suppress feelings of revulsion when the wart-faced, pink-eyed, clawed-hand goblin came too close. I noticed my friend's mate and the two little 'uns among the crowd cheering as loud as the rest. No jealousy there.

We'd only walked a few yards when a red carpet appeared under our feet and the cheers increased. I looked more closely at my neighbors and noticed that they came from many castes—leprechaun, dwarf, goblin, and gnome—but there were no princely representatives. We seemed to be playing the noble role for the night.

As we walked, the elementals broke ranks and followed us, pushing aside their neighbors to get a better view. But they soon tired and we were left alone. The show over, I gently disengaged my arm and waited for my friend to speak.

"They like to get a bit of play out of the human and that was a perfect opportunity," he mused.

"I couldn't agree more," I replied. "I'd much rather meet some of them in the daylight with you at my side than by myself."

Raising his eyebrow, he assessed me again and commented, "I'm always amazed at how some elementals terrify humans, just by their looks."

"It's not just their looks, it's also their energy. Some feel malevolent to me," said I, correcting his assessment.

"I understand what you're saying," agreed the leprechaun, "but if humans kept their egos strong, none of those elementals could affect them. The problem arises when humans are afraid and their egos collapse. This allows goblins to enter their aura and steal their life energy."

As he spoke, a dark cloud crossed over the setting sun, causing me to draw in. I felt my aura collapse in just the way he had described and reflected on how much more vulnerable people were to the entry of malevolent beings and thoughts, in the dark.

Following my thinking, my friend remarked, "In the bath we were speaking of the taboos in the elemental world about sharing our sexual energy with other castes. Now I'd like to discuss with you what we are allowed to do. We are allowed to share our energy through touch and also through our eyes, ears, and voices. The strongest of us can also do this through our thoughts, just as you do. When you and I were in the bath together, our energies flowed through the water to each other. Your mind is so strong that you can just think of your energy going to someone and it goes. This is not only because of your strong mind but also because you are a healer."

I had long known the truth of what the leprechaun said. Often when I conducted workshops, people came up and said that they felt I had been talking directly to them. I had also noticed that I could feel people's headaches and discomfort in their bodies, even if they didn't tell me about them. And if people did tell me of an ache, then I felt the energy leaving me and going to heal them.

We were walking slowly towards the village as I reflected on the properties of positive energy. As I turned my thoughts to the effects of negative energy, the leprechaun interrupted.

"What do you mean by negative energy?" he asked.

"I was thinking of some of the goblins and gnomes on this lane who want to take my energy. They feel greedy and malevolent. Do they have any positive effect on others and the world?" I asked.

"Do you think you humans are so different? Hitler and others like him have killed millions of people, but they were physically attractive so humans did not see their malevolence. In our world we look the way we are. There are no more malevolent elementals than there are humans," the leprechaun said huffily, defending his fellow-elementals.

"Good point, but is there a positive purpose for beings in both worlds stealing energy from other life forms?" I queried, unwilling to let the matter drop until I fully understood.

"Of course there is," he asserted in his teaching voice. "When either elementals or humans stand up to those who steal the light from the world, they strengthen their egos. They move one step closer to becoming creators. Depriving the evil ones of energy shrinks them so that they are forced to go to weaker beings to steal their energy. If there are no weaker ones, then in order to live they must start to think positive thoughts and do positive things in the world to draw energy to them."

My friend's words echoed those of a Cherokee teacher with whom I studied. From him I had learned that we seek tyrants to teach us a lesson. We may have unresolved issues with anger, self-pity, fear, greed, or lust. If so, we draw to us those people who trigger these reactions so that we can strengthen our ego and overcome our weakness. Although not free of these vices, I had a deeper issue relating to fear and reluctance in using my own power. Much of my fear had come from past lives in which I had been killed, burned at the stake, etcetera, for using my gifts.

Still, I could remember several times when my warrior spirit emerged to defend people who were attacked by malevolent beings. On one occasion a few years back I had been invited by a friend to a talk given by a well-known personal transformation organization. Having politely resisted all attempts by the converted to be signed up for the course, I had been left alone. Standing quietly off to one side, I noticed the main speaker of the evening attacking a young woman.

"You're fucked up. If you don't sign up you'll never get your life together," he was saying vehemently. The young woman was devastated by his words and tears streamed down her cheeks.

At that moment, the man turned and saw me watching. A look of hatred crossed his face. He stormed over, enraged that I had witnessed his behavior, and proceeded to attack me verbally. Immediately I felt a shield surround me, protecting me from his attack. Then a powerful energy moved up my spine, boosting my aura. With unshakable certainty and strength, I responded to the tyrant's accusations and said, "If you think this, you don't know me." His eyes were unable to meet mine and he quickly moved away in search of weaker prey.

I then walked to the woman in tears and tried to repair the damage he had done. Her energy field was full of holes, caused by his verbal missiles, through which her energy was rapidly leaking. Many of these "cults" are dangerous. They seek to destroy people's egos so that they can reprogram them according to the beliefs of the cult.

"We're here!" the leprechaun announced, his voice pulling me out of my inner thoughts. I looked up to find that we had arrived at The Unicorn—and that my friend had suddenly disappeared.

CHAPTER ELEVEN

Eating Out

THE UNICORN WAS AN OLD-FASHIONED, family-owned establishment. It had only one floor, like so many cheap motels in North America, but there the resemblance ended. Perched on the cliff overlooking the sea, its thick stone walls had been weathered by the harsh gales and storms blowing in from the Atlantic. Painted white, with roses clinging to the entrance, its massive door opened into a sunroom used for lunches and teas on summer days. At the far end was another large door, leading to the dining-room. I pulled it open and its loudly squeaking hinges announced my arrival. All heads turned to examine the single woman out for dinner.

I let out my breath and, looking around, saw my leprechaun friend seated at a table for two next to the fire. He waved to me. The other diners resumed eating, and a dark-haired colleen with a broad smile approached from my right. "Dinner for one?" she asked, with a voice that turned speaking into music.

"Yes," I replied as she led me towards the very table the leprechaun had chosen. She leaned forward to remove the other table setting and I exclaimed, "That's all right, you can leave it."

Giving me an indulgent "foreigners-have-strange-habits" look, she graced me with her lovely smile and inquired, "Would you like a drink before dinner?"

My friend nodded wildly, but I could think of no plausible way of ordering two glasses of wine without becoming the talk of the

77

village. Pausing to consider, I replied, "I'll wait a moment, thanks."

Hardly waiting for her departure, my friend confronted me, "Was that really necessary?"

"I'm happy to get you a drink," I answered him telepathically, defending my action. "I'm just trying to figure out how to do it inconspicuously. Any ideas?"

"Sure. Order half a bottle and pour us both a glassful," he retorted.

"You know these folks only see one person here," I said. "What will they think of me pouring two glasses?"

"The problem with you is that you always worry about what others will think. Just do it!" he said, egging me on.

Just then the colleen returned. "Are you ready to order?" she inquired with her friendly smile.

"A half-bottle of white wine, please," I responded and, opening the menu, continued, "I'll order dinner in a minute."

She left to get the wine and my leprechaun beamed approval.

Looking up from the menu, I told him, "I'd just like to make it clear that I'm not going to make a dinner out of things that never lived, just for your benefit. I intend to eat anything I want tonight."

For once he didn't speak, so I returned to the menu and decided on grilled salmon, potatoes, and asparagus. A tinkling in my wine glass alerted me to the colleen's return. Pausing, she waited patiently for me to sample the wine.

Savoring the first sip, I pronounced, "Delicious."

Smiling, she filled the rest of the glass, took my order, and left. Sitting across from me, the leprechaun was wringing his hands trying to restrain himself.

I filled his glass, saluted him with mine, and proffered the Irish toast, "Slainte."

Lifting his glass, he began sipping his wine as I had done, but got carried away and downed half of it. "UMMM! That's good," he pronounced contentedly, leaning back into his chair and putting his glass down on the table. My clairvoyance must have improved because I could see the difference in energy between his wine and mine. Now that he had taken half of his, my wine appeared more vibrant.

"I want to try an experiment with you," he suggested good-naturedly. "I will overlay my thoughts and feelings on yours when you're eating so that you can see why it's repulsive to us to eat beings who have been killed."

"What a splendid idea," I responded sarcastically. "That's exactly what I'd like on my special night out. You'll be pleased to hear that whenever I think of the being I'm eating, I do feel repulsed and nauseated. However, my body craves more than oats, fruit, and seeds."

I was interrupted by the colleen, bearing a gigantic plate of salmon and bowls of potatoes and vegetables. Her eye caught the second glass of wine and she looked at me questioningly.

"Oh, that's for the little people," I responded, winking mischievously.

She giggled in response, thoroughly enjoying my joke, and added as she turned to leave, "Why, of course."

Wine taken care of, I pointed at the celery, carrots, asparagus, and potatoes and asked my friend, "Which ones would you like to have?"

"Some potatoes, asparagus, and bread and butter, please," he replied, eyeing the food.

After transferring some vegetables onto my side plate and pushing them towards him, I began to devour my food with the relish of one too long deprived.

"The salmon's superb," I managed between mouthfuls. "How's your meal?"

"Excellent," my friend replied, his knife and fork firmly gripped in Irish fashion. Totally absorbed by the process of eating like a human, the leprechaun remained silent, allowing me to enjoy my meal. I was just savoring the last morsels when the colleen returned.

"Finished?" she asked. I snuck a peek at my friend to check his progress. The napkin was rubbing his mouth and cheeks while his hands lay across his ample belly. His eyes beamed at me mischievously and I saw images of immense desserts thrust into my mind.

"Yes, thank you," I replied to the waitress, "and I think we'll . . . I mean I'll . . . have dessert."

"There's apple pie, lemon sponge pudding, and treacle tart," she said.

Glancing across the table, I saw, dangling in midair, an immense piece of cake with a lemon sitting on top.

"Lemon sponge, please," I said, now smiling as broadly as she.

"Well done, well done," the leprechaun exclaimed after she left. Some neighboring diners rose to leave, nodding pleasantly in my direction. I was grateful that they did not come over to start a conversation, as I was enjoying the company of my friend.

After a few minutes our waitress returned with the pudding. Though not quite as large as the one conjured up by the leprechaun's imagination, it was enough for us both. I cut it down the middle with my spoon and moved the bowl into the middle of the table. He ate from his side and I from mine. We finished at the same time and I was certain he had slowed down for me.

"Thank you for a lovely evening, Tanis," he said, and disappeared. The waitress was approaching with the bill when I realized that this was the first time he had called me by name.

CHAPTER TWELVE

The Naming Day

T'S TIME YOU GOT UP," came a distant voice. From my dream of sunny beaches I was dragged back into the reality of another grey Irish day.

"Just a few more minutes," I pleaded, pulling the covers over my head.

"No. Now," the leprechaun asserted. "This is an important day. It's a naming day."

Surfacing, I opened one eye and was amazed to see the room covered in balloons and streamers. The leprechaun stood before me, dressed like a birthday package. He wore gold lamé pants and a blood-red velvet waistcoat. His favorite top hat was adorned with a gigantic green shamrock, and a large ribbon incorporating the gold, red, and green of his clothes was tied around his throat in a big bow.

"Because you have been furthering my education about humans, I am going to share with you the most important thing a leprechaun can." My friend bowed formally, paused for emphasis, and said, "My name." Then resuming his usual abrupt manner, he added, "So get up."

He turned and left the room. Amazed by what he had said, I threw back the covers and began to dress rapidly. It was common knowledge in folklore that if a leprechaun told you his name you could control him. Well, I'd soon find out the truth about that, I thought, smiling to myself at the likelihood that my friend would ever willingly let me control him.

Just as I finished dressing and entered the living room, my friend returned, carrying a beautiful book. It was white and gleamed with gold letters. He carried it reverently, without any of his normal mocking manner, and it was plain to see that today he was being genuinely serious.

Seating himself on the couch beside me, he began, "This is my book of names. It holds all the memories of who I am and what I've done and will do."

I waited for him to continue.

Opening the book at random, he said, "Here's the time when I decided to leave my traditional caste to study humans."

He was about to go on when, unable to contain my curiosity, I interrupted, "What was your traditional caste?"

The leprechaun's right eyebrow arched slightly in disapproval, but then he laughed. "You remind me of my little 'uns. Questions, questions."

"So are you going to tell me?" I persisted good-humoredly.

"I'm of the leprechaun caste, of course!" he said proudly.

"But aren't there any subgroups—like shoemakers and tailors?"

"Oh, I see what you mean," he said. "Aye, leprechauns do those kinds of work and also some of us are jewelers, but it's mostly the dwarves who work with metal. I probably would have done clothes for special occasions, if I'd had to choose, but something steered my path in a different direction."

With those words he leaned towards me and said in a conspiratorial tone, "I met a human."

"I don't understand," I said. "Don't you see humans every day?"

Chuckling, he responded, "Our own world is quite interesting enough without venturing into yours. Haven't you noticed how seldom you see my mate and little 'uns? That's because they're staying in our own world.

"Not only that," he continued, "but there are more worlds than just these two—yours and mine—that we can visit."

He raised his hand to deflect my inevitable question and said with a smile, "No, no, no. We'll deal with that another day. Let's get back to the human I met.

"He was visiting our world and doing research on our life. I was young, still not a grownup, and was hanging around scholars trying to glean bits and pieces of information. That was already considered somewhat unusual in our world, but sometimes leprechauns become scholars. Although usually scholars come from a different caste. They're. . . ."

"As you were saying, the human. . . ." I interrupted, attempting to get him back on track. I could tell that we were still a long way off from talking about his name.

"Oh, aye, the human," he continued, straightening his waistcoat. "The human noticed me noticing him and started moving towards me. I was terrified. Since we were little 'uns we had been told stories about how humans stole our energy and killed the world. Still, I didn't move. As he came closer he got larger and larger—about the same height as our noble caste, but denser and heavier. He had dark black hair and wore a black cape. He had the look of a magician about him, very smart and very powerful.

"'Hello, young one,' he greeted me.

"'I'm not so young!' I replied, insulted as only the young can be.

"Jerking back his head, he laughed, showing the gold in his teeth and then, laughter still in his eyes, he asked, 'Have you decided what path to take in life?'

"Well!" Turning to me, the leprechaun spoke in whispers, "In the elemental world this question is never asked. It would be considered a kind of shame if others knew that I was considering that question, so I was embarrassed to have been found out.

"He seemed to read my thoughts, something I didn't think humans could do, and said, 'Times are changing, young one. I've been talking with your elder scholars about getting together a group of elementals from all castes to work with humans. We are looking for ones who think for themselves and have curiosity and courage. Interested?'

"I didn't know at that time that our new caste would first be ridiculed and then feared by our fellow elementals, or I might not have gone. Still, I knew that I'd come to an important fork in my life path where I had to make some choices. Pulling myself up to my full height, I looked the human in the eye and said, 'Aye, I'd like to try that.'

"That was almost a hundred years ago," my friend said, settling back in the couch. Now quite a few elementals know about our work with humans, and we have young 'uns applying to join us. Also we know that the true purpose of our caste is to learn to become conscious creators like you humans."

"That's an incredible story," I said, amazed. "Has this got anything to do with you telling me your name?"

"Just everything," he giggled, putting his hands over his stomach and rolling around the couch.

I knew that he was laughing at my cleverness in guessing this. Sometimes I forgot that he and I were of very different species, and it took moments like this to remind me. I waited calmly for him to regain his composure.

Watching me watching him just set him off again, and then I was laughing with him. We were like two kids and maybe not so different after all.

Slowly he steadied himself. He removed his top hat to reveal a shock of bright-red hair standing out all over his head. Putting his hat in his lap, he began, "Before I tell you my name, I'm going to tell you about names."

"Oh, oh. Here we go on another digression," I thought as quietly as I could.

If he heard me, he pretended not to and continued, "Most of you humans don't even know your right names, so you don't know who you really are."

Immediately I started to wonder if my name was right for me. It had always felt right until this minute. My parents told me that they had been lying in bed when my mother was eight months pregnant and that my father had heard my name, Tanis. Neither one of them knew a Tanis, but they had heard the name before in connection with family friends.

My name has always been a signpost for me. As a child I learned that my name was Cree Indian and meant "my daughter." Later, as an adult, a Cree man told me that Tanis was a special name to his people and meant both a daughter to the whole tribe and a gift from the creator. In the last few years, other meanings for my name have been revealed. The ancient city of Tanis was located in the delta of Egypt and was the capital during the reign of Ramses II. It was located in the crown chakra of Egypt. Also, in the Bible, Tanis was called Zoan and was the place where the righteous people fled after the destruction of Sodom and Gomorrah.

My leprechaun friend was following my thoughts and said, "Your name is your correct one. That is what a name really should be for people. It should be their identity."

"Often I meet people," I replied, "and forget their names because they don't seem right. In fact, sometimes I even call them by different names."

"You may be calling them by their right names, Tanis," he replied.

"Is there anything else you want to tell me about my name before we talk about yours?" I said, teasing.

"We'll get to mine in a minute, but I'd like to tell you why elementals won't tell their name," he offered, increasing the suspense.

"I'd love to hear that," I said, with mock seriousness.

"First of all," he commenced, "we don't get a name when we're born, like you humans. We need to grow into our names. It's not until we have enough life experience and we can remember our story that we get to choose our name. Then the elders have to agree that we have chosen the right one."

Listening to him, I was reminded of similarities in human society. "In some Native tribes," I said, "children are given one name when they're born and they choose another for themselves on a vision quest at puberty. Then, some very special individuals are given a name by the tribe if they have done great things. The Native way and your way seem to make much more sense to me than the conventional human process. Being named at birth by people who don't have any connection to your spiritual essence seems inappropriate. And the individual is stuck with that name for life.

"So I understand the importance of names, but why do elementals not reveal theirs?" I inquired, getting us back on track. "To my way of thinking it would strengthen their ego, which is what you say elementals need to do."

"That's true," he replied, "but elementals with a stronger ego would then know the life essence of the weaker one and would be able to control him. This is why we do not tell humans our name. If they were to call us and ask us for something, we could not refuse them."

"So why do you want to tell me your name," I asked. "I admit that I've wanted to know since the beginning, but I don't want to force you into anything against your will."

"That's exactly why I wish to share my name with you," the leprechaun said. "You have not once asked me to do anything against my will. Furthermore, there is great reluctance in your essence to do this to others."

"Is there anything to be gained for either of us in telling me your name?" I interjected quickly, before he could go further. I was becoming increasingly nervous about the responsibility of knowing it.

"You will see that when I speak it," he said and continued, "my name is Lloyd."

Nothing happened. Not a thing. "Your name is not Lloyd," I stated with certainty. "Tell me your real name," I commanded.

Softly, the leprechaun said his real name and, as he did, a gate opened between us. Our two energies flowed towards each other from the center of our hearts and merged. As this happened, I could feel the pull of other dimensions, other realities, opening to me. I knew that I could go through the gate to explore them, but the time did not feel right. I pulled back and closed my part of the gate.

The leprechaun's energy hung sparkling in the air for a moment and then was reabsorbed into his body. He sat looking at me, wise, kind, and utterly different from the mischievous being I had come to know. As I watched, he pulled his energy even further into his aura and became again his impish self.

"You see, now that I have shared my name with you, we can go into other realms together," he said, smiling.

"Why did you want me to command you?" I said, knowing that it had been expected of me.

"It's necessary in name-sharing ceremonies for the two beings to match each other's energy. You normally hold your energy in too tightly for fear of upsetting others, and you try to take up less space. In this case, you had to take up your real power."

"Thank you for your gift," I said.

"Our gift," he corrected.

"Am I allowed to tell anyone your name?" I asked, not wanting to make any errors.

"More on that tomorrow," he said and started to disappear.

"One more question," I called after him. "Who was the human you met almost a hundred years ago?"

"Steiner. Rudolph Steiner," came the faint echo.

CHAPTER THIRTEEN

Secrets

'VE NEVER UNDERSTOOD WHY PEOPLE LIKE SECRETS. As a therapist, I've kept lots of secrets for people—secrets that are not mine to share. But the secrets of life—the inner mysteries—are secrets I am driven to share with as many people as care to listen.

Of course, this is what got Jesus killed. He told the secrets of the inner mysteries in parable form while proclaiming, "Let those who have an ear to hear, hear." At that time, however, it was forbidden to speak of the mysteries to the uninitiated and so the Rabbis made short order of Jesus, the betrayer of their secrets.

I was pondering the nature of the leprechaun's secret the next morning, sitting on the couch with my usual cup of tea. Was it a secret to be shared or kept to myself?

"Well, that's a big topic," said my leprechaun friend, flopping down onto the couch and reaching for the cup of tea I had poured for him.

Holding the cup in both hands and sipping the hot tea, he continued, "I thought we would discuss the importance of humans' last names before talking about secrets."

"Our last names announce our ancestry," I responded, "indicating whether we carry English, German, or Japanese blood. In some cases, our names even give insight into our talents or those of our ancestors.

"For example, my name, Helliwell, is the balance between the light and dark aspects—the conscious world of the sun and the unconscious world of the moon. It says a lot about who I am and what I do. I don't understand why women take their husband's name when they marry, because that name has nothing to do with them genetically."

The leprechaun listened attentively, then asked, "Why do children take their father's and not their mother's name?"

"It used to be that children took their mother's names," I replied. "This makes sense, as we can be sure of who our mother is, but less sure of the father. But men didn't like this. They saw women and children as their possessions and wanted to put their stamp of ownership on both."

"In our world," the leprechaun interjected, "as we evolve, our women have children just as you humans do. My mate carried our two children in her body. When we look at an elemental or a human, we can immediately see who their mother, father, and even other ancestors are. It's written all over their vibration. Therefore, we don't need to have a last name."

Pausing to reconsider, he added, "Sometimes however, we list the person's talent or fame after their name. Like, for example, Robin the Hood, of Sherwood Forest."

He sat back and smirked at his ability to identify human folk heroes.

I found myself wondering if Robin Hood was connected to the elemental world, and projected my thought towards him.

"We have our own version of the story—the true one," volunteered my leprechaun friend. "It concerns a noble faery prince whose father left him in charge of the kingdom while he went off to war. The father's brother insinuated himself into the court by guile and threw out the innocent prince. Prince Robin escaped to the forest where he was befriended by the birds and animals. Meanwhile the evil uncle brought unhappiness and despair to the kingdom. Other noble faery men fled to Robin and together they fought the uncle, retreating to the shelter of the forest to hide. Finally the king returned, and his kingdom was restored."

"Humans seem to have a lot of stories based on the faery world," I observed. "Do you take stories from us as well?"

"Most of your stories depress us," he replied candidly. "Think of Dickens, Shakespeare, and Dostoyevsky and you'll see what I mean. The themes of these stories are the reasons for us not associating with humans. Our favorite human stories are ones we've helped to write, such as Lewis Carroll's *Alice in Wonderland* and C.S. Lewis's Narnia series."

I had a sudden insight that I wanted to confirm. "Stories are not just for entertainment, are they?" I asked. "They are records of human consciousness—not just for an individual, but for our race. Stories are like names; they are stamps saying who we are."

"Absolutely!" he exclaimed.

"For years," I continued, "I've resisted reading the newspaper or watching the news on television. I find these media not only depressing but obscene. They seem to strengthen the concept that our world is a mess and build a negative thought-form of violence. That's exactly what's happening, isn't it?"

"Absolutely!" he exclaimed again.

"The problem is," I said, frustrated, "that apart from saying to others what I've just said to you, I don't know what else to do about it. Do you have any ideas?"

"Absolutely!" he cried for the third time. "You must tell a different story. Tell people about us and keep supporting others who are supporting the Earth and all life on it."

"Are you suggesting that I write a book about you, or teach courses?" I asked, feeling responsibility claim me.

"All of the above, but with a light and joyful spirit," he said, smiling at me.

"That covers names and stories," I said, knowing how his circuitous mind worked. "Surely we must be leading back to secrets."

"Aye, secrets," said my friend in hushed tones, glancing melodramatically over his shoulder, as if to see who was watching. As he rolled his eyes from side to side and held his finger to his lips, I heard a ghostly *ssshhhh* echo through the room. I smiled, thoroughly enjoying his impish humor. Obviously secrets weren't sacred—thank goodness.

His laughter subsiding, he stood up and started walking back and forth across the room, rubbing his chin. The philosopher had returned.

"There are secrets and secrets," he started, looking up at me with one arched eyebrow.

I nodded, so far in agreement, and waited.

"This is a dilemma," he said, continuing to pace the room.

I waited, suspense growing.

Stopping dead in his tracks, he turned and said, "I'll be back in a minute," and disappeared.

This was an interesting turn of events—a first, to be sure. The leprechaun was unsure of himself and was going to ask his superiors, I guessed. I poured a lukewarm cup of tea and waited.

Seconds turned to minutes. A really serious topic, I thought, finishing the last of the tea.

"There be secrets and there be secrets, me hearty," came his disembodied voice.

"I don't have to tell anyone your name," I said as he appeared and sat down. "I can just call you the leprechaun."

"We were just discussing that and have decided that that's best," he responded.

My heart sank. The first question anyone was going to ask me was, "What's his name?" Not being able to reveal it was not conducive to building up trust and credibility in my story—the story that he wanted me to tell. I liked it better when I didn't know his name so that I could be in the same boat as everyone else.

"But you're not everyone else," he reminded me. "You can teach people how to meet their own elementals and they can ask them their names. You can't tell mine to everyone for one very good reason."

"Which is?" I said, prompting him to continue.

"Which is that I don't want thousands of people calling on me to teach them about elementals," he replied. "I haven't got enough strength to do that and they'll just take me off my path."

"I understand perfectly," I said. "In fact, I agree with you. And that's the very reason I don't know if I want to become well known in any area, even about leprechauns. I'm afraid that people will lock me into that one area and I'll no longer be able to explore all the different aspects of learning that I enjoy."

"There's an easy solution to that," he responded smugly. "You just have to make sure that the area you choose is broad enough.

"Oh, like talking to faeries," I said, folding my arms across my chest.

"You've got a point," he agreed grudgingly.

"Have you any ideas how I can keep the area broad enough so that I won't get bored?" I asked. "Fascinating though you are, I don't know if I want to spend the rest of my life doing workshops on elementals."

"I've got the perfect solution," he replied. "Don't write this book for ten years. By that time you will be well established both in the corporate world and in the field of spiritual teaching, and most important, it will also be the right time for the world to hear our message."

"And will it be the right time for your name to be given?" I asked, hopefully.

"Maybe, but it's unlikely," he said, chuckling. "Time in our two worlds is different. I don't think my ego identity will be strong enough in ten years, but yours will be. You will not have to worry about being taken off your path; this will only reinforce your direction."

"Okay, I agree," I said, "but is there some name I could use for you instead of your real name?"

"'Fraid not," he replied. "Any name has power, and if people call me by the wrong name they will start to take my energy away from my real one."

"Does that mean that I have to call you the leprechaun for the entire book?" I asked, mouthing the words, "Bor-ring."

"Yup," the leprechaun said, stifling a yawn and starting to disappear.

"One more question," I asked quickly.

"'One more question' is getting to be a habit with you," he said, resolidifying. "Well, what is it?" he said, feigning annoyance.

"Who did you talk to about this secrecy issue when you disappeared?" I asked.

"Tomorrow," he said, smiling and started to fade. His smile was the last part to disappear.

CHAPTER FOURTEEN

Church and the Pub

AYS CAME AND WENT, with no leprechaun. The end of my month at the cottage was fast approaching and I seemed to be no further ahead on my spiritual pilgrimage. I'd done a lot of meditating when not entertaining my elemental friend, and I was still not enlightened.

A traveling bookmobile arrived at the village one morning while I was grocery shopping, and I decided that some light reading would brighten up my lonely days. Having finished Dante's *Inferno* and both Matthew and Luke of The New Testament, I was ready for some science fiction. Thinking just that, I walked up the wobbly steps of the old van to browse through the selection.

"Good day. Can I help you?" I was greeted by a cheerful attractive man who looked more like a cross between a soccer player and a fisherman than a librarian. He had the tanned healthy look of someone who worked outdoors, combined with the physical grace of someone fully in tune with his body.

"Would I be allowed to take out some books?" I inquired.

"Of course, just as long as you bring them back. I come every two weeks and park here for two hours," he replied, smiling, and continued, "You're allowed five books."

Eyes now accustomed to the dim light, I saw rows of books stacked on either side of the van. "I'll just look around first, if you don't mind," I responded.

"Not at all. Just call if you need assistance," he replied, turning to the next customer coming up the steps.

Moving through the shelves filled with biographies and picture books on the origin of our star system, I searched for science fiction. There were lots of love stories, which I imagined were in hot demand by the women of these remote towns. However, I could find no science fiction books at all.

Momentarily disappointed, I absentmindedly picked up the book on our star system. Maybe it would help deepen my understanding of some of the passages in *Decoding Destiny,* I thought. As I turned the pages, my eye caught sight of the children's section. There, a large book protruded over the edge of the shelf. *Fairies,* it said. Reaching over, I picked it up and opened it at random. A large picture of a leprechaun stared back at me. Perfect, I thought. I'll get it for the little 'uns—they'll love it.

Picking up my bag of groceries, I checked out the two books and strolled back up the lane to the cottage. Walking in the door, I saw the little 'uns waiting for me beside the dining room table. They knew full well what I'd brought them. I put down the groceries and carried the faery book to the table. They jumped up and down and kept pushing each other out of the way to get a better view. Because books did not exist in their realm they had never seen pictures of elementals before and were fascinated that humans had recorded them. They behaved like children discovering a mirror for the first time. Opening the book to the first page, I said, "I'll turn the page every day so you can see another elemental."

They leaned over and had a look at a goblin that looked very similar to the one on our lane. Pointing to its long nose, they giggled and chattered excitedly. Their voices were so light and quick that I couldn't really make out what they were saying. It didn't take them long to tire of the picture, but just before the older one disappeared, he looked back at me and smiled his thanks.

Every day thereafter, I opened the book to the next page and sometime during the day discovered the little 'uns looking at the new picture. Two weeks later I renewed the book.

I was just putting away the groceries when I saw Mrs. O'Toole coming through the gate. A bit early, I thought, turning to open the door.

"Welcome," I said, stepping aside to wave her in. "You're just in time for some chocolate-covered biscuits."

"I can't stop today," she said, walking past me to the hearth where she proceeded to remove the cold ashes of the previous night.

Looking over her shoulder at me, eyes twinkling, she added, "We've mass tonight, and afterwards we're goin' to the pub. Would you like to come?"

"I'd love to," was out of my mouth instantly.

The turf stacked, she lit it and said, "Maureen will pick you up at seven-thirty."

Mrs. O'Toole strolled past me out the door. Congratulating myself on my good fortune, I glanced at my watch and saw that I had three hours in which to get ready. It was weeks since I had last gone out with company, and I planned to enjoy it thoroughly.

Promptly at seven-thirty, Maureen arrived. Like me she was dressed in a skirt, blouse, and sweater. I had the Queen Elizabeth kerchief tucked in my purse should it be needed but was relieved to see that Maureen was bareheaded. The car was parked at the gate and the kids were dressed in their Sunday best.

I greeted Brendan, Shannon, and Bridget, and we set off. Located between two towns, the church was a large white building surrounded by dozens of cars and bicycles. I found it fascinating that there were four pubs in my village alone, but only one church between two, or maybe three, villages.

Brendan parked the car and everyone leapt out. I fell into line behind the girls and watched Maureen like a hawk to make sure that I did everything right. Not only was I not Catholic but I was almost sure that there'd be some small village Irish Catholic idiosyncrasies in the mass that I'd have to follow. At the basin of holy water at the entrance, Maureen, Brendan, and the girls dipped their fingers and crossed themselves on the forehead. I followed suit.

Nodding to all the neighbors as she walked up the aisle, Maureen saw her mom and dad and sat down beside them. I joined them, noticing Mrs. O'Toole a few seats away. She had on a clean flowered dress and sweater, with not a safety pin in sight. Her wellies had been replaced by stockings and sturdy shoes. Her kerchief had been removed to reveal a head of shiny brown hair, liberally streaked with grey. She looked a decade younger.

I was trying to get a good look at Mr. O'Toole when I realized that Maureen's family had dropped to their knees and were busy praying. I knelt hurriedly but no sooner had my knees touched the hard wooden bench at my feet when I heard them get up again. I slid back onto my seat as inconspicuously as possible. Opening my eyes, I glanced across the aisle and caught sight of two families watching me. I smiled. They smiled. They looked down. I looked down. Everyone knew I was the stranger in town and would be watching me for any strange foreign behavior.

Maureen held her rosary in her hand and, looking around, I observed that almost everyone did. I quickly reached into my purse and pulled out my grandmother's. Grandma, on my mother's side, had been an Irish Catholic (who later converted to Presbyterianism) and had left me her rosary. I was proud of Grandma. She had been raised on a farm with seven other children by a mother who died early and a father who drank too much. All her brothers and sisters had died young, but Grandma had survived until her ninety-second year.

Grandma was one of the best living people I've ever met. She was good-humored and loving and never spoke badly of anyone. She was tolerant and hard-working, and I loved her. Since her death I had slept every night on her plastic rosary and, although I had no idea how to count Hail Marys, I was comforted by it.

I was startled out of my memories by the organ calling us to attention. The entire congregation stood as the priest entered near the altar. He commenced the mass with a few words and the congregation responded. Although prayer books were provided, everyone seemed to know most of the mass by heart. It was quite similar to the United Church service with which I was familiar, with ritual responses substituted for hymns. Also, there were many more prayers to Mary and fewer to Jesus. Protestants don't pray to Mary, but including her always seemed to me to be a better balance of the male and female aspects of Christianity.

The priest was uninspiring but seemed a perfect fit for his parish. Middle-aged and conservative, he knew the mass perfectly and was faithful to the letter of the scripture.

The collection finished, we moved to the last part of the mass—the communion. I wanted to participate but wondered if the priest might object if he knew that I was Protestant. I had no wish to offend or deceive him, but receiving communion was for the greater good, and so I stood up and joined the line.

Walking slowly to the front, I watched people crossing themselves before receiving the wafer. When my turn came, I knelt and followed their example. Returning to my seat, I closed my eyes and prayed for all beings on the Earth. I prayed for the ability to love and better serve all sentient beings. Yes, taking communion had been the right thing to do.

The priest said his closing words and, dismissed, we faced the altar, genuflected, and left the church. It was nine o'clock and time for the pub. Following the girls into the back seat of the car, I was surprised when Mrs. O'Toole sidled in beside me.

"Paddy's gone ahead to get a table and Brendan will drop us off," she said by way of explanation.

Paddy, I assumed, was Mr. O'Toole, to whom I had not yet been formally introduced.

Brendan started up the motor and said over his shoulder, "We'll not be goin' to the pub tonight. I've got a practice with the boys."

"The boys?" I said, not understanding.

"Football," he said. I made a quick translation and remembered that football in Ireland was what we called soccer in North America. Maureen said nothing, but I surmised that she'd be taking the girls home to bed.

Brendan took off at his usual breakneck speed, and I mentally crossed myself. Minutes later we screeched to a halt at the bottom of my lane in front of the pub. There were already a lot of cars parked outside. On the door was a big sign—"Music tonight."

Mrs. O'Toole and I hastily got out, thanked Brendan for the lift, and entered the pub. The room was packed and buzzed with laughter and animated conversation. Squinting my eyes through the smoke, I saw a small man waving to us from a far table. He had two free chairs vacant beside him. A miracle. I headed towards him and Mrs. O'Toole sauntered along behind. Everyone looked surprised to see her and nodded to her warmly in recognition. She smiled shyly and nodded back.

I sat down on the chair farthest from Mr. O'Toole, leaving the one nearest him vacant for his wife. I got the feeling that they didn't get out much for a night together and was touched that they would share the occasion with me.

"This is Paddy," Mrs. O'Toole said by way of introduction. Mr. O'Toole extended a rough well-weathered hand to shake. His knuckles were enlarged by rheumatism and years of use, but his grip was firm. He was a small man with a slight frame. His black cap topped off a rosy face with twinkling eyes and a warm smile. Both he and Mrs. O'Toole radiated the same kind, wholesome goodness that I've often noticed among those who live close to the land.

"Could I get you a drink?" Mr. O'Toole asked courteously.

"A shandy please," I replied.

"And you, mother?" he inquired lovingly of Mrs. O'Toole.

"Lemon squash."

As he left I noticed that he was limping. Mrs. O'Toole, following my gaze, leaned over and said, "He's a bad hip and will be gettin' a replacement next year."

"How old is Mr. O'Toole?" I inquired.

"Sixty-five," she replied.

I was amazed, having seen this man riding his bike all times of the day and in all kinds of weather to visit his cows and sheep. He acted like a much younger man, in spite of his bad hip.

Returning with our drinks and a pint of black Guinness for himself, he sat down.

"Thank you," I said to his lowered head, and asked him about his farm. When he didn't respond, Mrs. O'Toole, observing my confusion, looked over and said, "Hard of hearin'—damaged in the war."

We were saved from the embarrassment of trying to communicate by the entrance of the musicians. There was no stage and the players seated themselves unpretentiously on chairs, just two tables down from us.

The music started up and the conversation lessened a little as people listened. One musician played the pipes—an instrument, I learned that summer, that was invented in Ireland, not Scotland. Another played a bodrum, an Irish hand drum that was played using both ends of a stubby stick. It looked difficult. The third musician was playing a guitar and had something that looked like a banjo on a stand beside him.

The music was good and Mr. O'Toole began to tap his feet to the beat. Before long people were singing along. In between songs a local girl got up and whispered something in the guitar player's ear. He started playing a song that she sang to a loudly appreciative audience.

The band took a break and, noticing that Mr. O'Toole's glass was empty, I caught his eye and said, in my best Irish idiom, "My shout. Do you want another Guinness?"

Surprised, he nodded and I made my way through the wall of bodies to the bar. Everyone seemed to know each other. Some of the men eyed me appraisingly. Not pushy, just curious. I saw a freckled-faced redhead looking at me more than once, but he quickly averted his eyes when I turned towards him. Shy. I like that, I said to myself, then quickly pushed the thought away. Meditation and leprechaun lessons were the focus of my summer—not redheaded Irishmen, I reminded myself. I got my drink and returned to Mr. and Mrs. O'Toole. Strange, but I just couldn't call either of them by their first name.

"Does everyone go to mass on Saturday evening instead of Sunday mornin'?" I asked Mr. O'Toole loudly, trying to start a conversation.

"Aye. That way we can go to the pub afterwards and sleep in Sunday morning," he replied, with a twinkle in his eye. Practical people, the Irish.

I could imagine how long he got to sleep in, with the cows needing to be milked. But before I could continue our conversation, the musicians returned and the music resumed. An hour or so later, our glasses empty, we looked at each other and agreed that we'd had enough. We left just as the bartender rang the bell announcing the last call before closing. Mr. O'Toole rode his bike up the lane and Mrs. O'Toole and I walked. It was a lovely night and I basked in the silence and fresh air, after the smoke and noise of the pub. I left Mrs. O'Toole at her gate and continued up the lane to my cottage. The embers still glowed faintly in the fireplace, welcoming me home.

CHAPTER FIFTEEN

My Body Elemental

HE LEPRECHAUN DID NOT APPEAR THE NEXT MORNING and I had a solitary, uneventful day. Sunday—a day of rest, I thought, getting undressed and into bed. I proceeded to do a nighttime meditation by candlelight—one of my disciplines to increase my concentration and confront any negative thought-forms.

Thoughtforms are created by thinking the same thoughts over and over again. They can be positive or negative, with almost a life of their own. Thoughtforms can be so strong that they affix themselves to other people. We therefore need to be careful with our thoughts, not only for ourselves, but also for others.

Sitting cross-legged, spine erect, I was exploring the seven deadly sins to see what thoughtforms I had created in those areas. I also wanted to identify the original good intention I had when creating them. I saw that lust had stemmed from wanting to be loved; that greed was rooted in a thirst for greater knowledge and experience; that envy was based in my desire to have everything that the creator could give; and that my slothfulness came from trusting that the creator would provide.

In my meditation, I called up my negative thoughtforms and reabsorbed them into the void of my body, dissolving them until they represented only the original positive intent. Then I fed my body the love, acceptance, abundance, and trust it needed. As I did this, I felt my body's resistance to accepting these gifts. It was as if it did not trust me. I was suddenly struck with the awareness that my body housed another being who was not me. It wasn't some separate entity either. Rather it was as if my mind and consciousness were distinct from some other consciousness connected to my body.

"Who are you?" I asked it.

Silence followed my question but I could sense something hovering in my internal shadows.

"I want to know who you are," I repeated, unwilling to give up. My consciousness became a flashlight searching the shadows to find the being who lived there. I felt it observing me, unwilling to be known. I could sense its feelings of distrust, resentment, resignation, and also curiosity and hope.

"I will not harm you. I really want to know you," I thought, sending it love.

Softly it replied, "I don't trust you. Go away and leave me alone to do my work."

The reference to work gave me a clue as to its purpose in my body, which I instinctively felt was positive. "What kind of work do you do?" I asked.

Silence again, accompanied by feelings of both hopelessness and hope.

"Please trust me," I said sincerely. "If I've done something to you it was because I didn't know you were there. Now that I know, things can be different. I need your help if I'm to understand what you want me to do."

It hesitated a bit longer and then responded.

"Very well," it said, "I don't think you'll do more harm knowing than not knowing me, so I'll tell you. I am your body elemental."

"My what?" I said, confused. "What is a body elemental?"

"You mean who is a body elemental!" it said, annoyed. I could feel it slipping into hopelessness again.

Quickly I interjected apologetically, "This is all new. Please excuse my ignorance and teach me about you and your work."

"It's not easy to sum up millions of years of work in a sentence," it mocked me.

"We've got the whole night," I replied, thinking a little humor might ease the tension.

"Your charm won't work on me like it works on that other elemental," he responded testily, projecting the image of my leprechaun friend.

Fresh out of approaches, I sighed and said, "I will not force you to tell me against your will. You must decide if it's good for me to understand who you are or not. I trust you even if you do not trust me."

My words were like an open sesame, because it immediately spewed forth eons of stored grievances against me.

"I've been with you from your very first incarnation as a human and you don't even know who I am," it stated angrily. "I'm the architect who builds your body every lifetime and incorporates all the strengths and wounds that you have acquired from each life. I stay in your body, making sure that everything keeps on working right up until you die. Only then," it said, pausing for breath, "do I get time off to rest before it's time for you to incarnate again."

There could be no doubt as to the truth of its words. All my cells acknowledged this. I was ashamed of my lack of appreciation, and ignorance no longer seemed like a good excuse. I allowed it to feel my dilemma and asked for direction.

Somewhat mollified, it continued grudgingly, "It's not just you. You're no worse than all the other humans who have no idea what we body elementals do for them. Without us they would not even be alive."

Searching for a solution, I suggested, "If you tell me what I could do to cooperate with you I could try to do that. Also I'd be happy to share your information with other humans."

Still not completely won over, it threw out a test question. "Have you ever thought about how an acorn knows to become an oak—not just any oak, but an oak that has two main branches, not four, and grows fifty feet tall, not sixty? An oak that has cankers growing on its trunk?"

Replaying my memories, I searched for this information before replying, "I probably would put it down to the soil and amount of water and sunlight, and how strong the seed was originally. Is that incorrect?"

"Not incorrect, but only part of the story," it replied, adding, "and that's all humans see."

"Well, I also know that there are tree devas and faeries and other kinds of elementals that watch over all growing things and help them to grow," I added quickly, to credit elementals with their gift to the Earth.

"That's more of the story, and more than most humans believe," it responded, "but the last part, of which you seem to be unaware, is the role of body elementals in growing all living things." Its voice was more sad than strident now.

"Then please teach me so that I can correct my ignorance," I asked humbly. "Perhaps then we can work together to achieve more cooperation between body elementals and humans for the good not only of humans but the world."

"That was the original intention," the body elemental replied, a touch of sarcasm in its voice. "I've heard you say many times that humans are like gods in training, and you're absolutely right, they are, but you cannot become creators without our full cooperation. Body elementals build what humans envision. If humans think or feel anything, it is our job to record that memory in their cells. Humans decide what it is that we are to record. If you cannot control negative emotions such as greed, anger, lust, gluttony, or fear, then these are what we record. We are architects and scribes for your body."

Suddenly I remembered that I had been replacing my own negative thoughtforms with their original positive seeds when I first noticed my body elemental. Could this be coincidence, I wondered.

"Not at all," it replied, hearing my thought. "In your journey towards becoming a creator, you are now taking responsibility for everything you have ever created. You are uncovering and erasing negative thoughts and memories from this life and all others. I have been assisting you in this process as it is my job to follow your commands."

"You don't exactly have the voice of a willing server," I said, letting my humor bubble to the surface.

This time it was not offended and responded, "What I am comes from you."

"Please continue," I urged, excited by the new avenue of knowledge opening up to me.

"Body elementals evolve in conjunction with their host," it said, sounding neither eager nor resistant in answering my questions. "Like other elementals, when we first start life we are empty—a blank slate except for our function. With each of your lives, you give us more memories to hold and we become more complex and conscious. In a way, I'm a mirror for you. Like you, I am strong-willed, fearful, curious, stubborn, loyal, wise, and also eager to help my fellow body elementals evolve to work consciously in the world."

Suddenly I realized that it was in its best interest to help me reprogram my body with positive thoughts and feelings. It would hasten its evolution as well as mine.

"You are absolutely correct," it said, "and this is why I decided to make myself known to you tonight. It is not without risk that I do so."

"What risk is there?" I asked, completely blank as to what it could be.

"Black magicians use their body elementals to create a double, which they send to harm others. When the double returns to the host the body elemental has to absorb the acts that the black magician willed the double to do. This greatly impedes the evolution of the body elemental. It is our psychic death."

Immediately I thought of the Carlos Castaneda books on psychic warfare and of British adepts who followed the black path in this way. I had experienced psychic attacks more than once and had a great respect for the power of the wills behind them, as well as a strong aversion to following this path myself.

"And that," the body elemental said, overhearing my thoughts, "is exactly why I've decided to make myself known to you. At some point in every being's evolution, we must start working together or it is impossible for them to become a creator. All great adepts, like Jesus the Christ and Gautama the Buddha, worked with their body elementals to create bodies for themselves after their physical death. Now it's time for us to work together."

"Right," I agreed willingly. "When do we start?"

"We've already started," the body elemental said, and I could feel a slight smile beneath the tough veneer. "When you work in accordance with the divine plan, as you do increasingly, then my work is both faster and stronger because it's in accordance with my ultimate programming."

"Any suggestions for improvement?" I asked, always eager to do better. "Working with all elementals," it replied, "as you are doing this summer, will strengthen our connection and be for the good of all beings developing on this planet. Body elementals build the form of the trees, flowers, minerals, animals, fish, birds—in fact, everything. Earth is a living being and we are the cells in its body. As each of us aligns itself to the divine plan, the entire planet does so as well."

"I agree," I said, supporting its position. "However, I'm still unclear about the differences between the function of body elementals and that of elementals like the faeries and devas of trees and mountains."

"I've already explained what body elementals do," it responded. "I think it would be better for you to speak directly with faeries and devas to learn what they do."

"Good point," I agreed, making a mental note to do so in the morning. I could feel myself starting to lose consciousness and was reluctant to take leave of my body elemental so soon.

"I'm always here and you can contact me whenever you like," it reassured me. "You can ask me to reprogram certain parts of your body that are out of balance. Also, you can talk to the body elementals of other humans, as you have done on many occasions. In this life, you do it instinctively because you have done it consciously in other lives. You can access those memories, should you wish."

As it spoke, I could sense such memories on the edge of my awareness, but I was too tired to proceed. The candles had long ago burned out. Sliding down in my bed, I mentally thanked my body elemental and instantly fell asleep.

CHAPTER SIXTEEN

The Old Ones

HE NEXT DAY THE LEPRECHAUN REAPPEARED. Coming back from an early morning walk and still in my nightie under my raincoat, I walked into the cottage and saw my friend hovering over the faery book, explaining the various pictures to his two children. They followed with rapt attention.

Glad to see him, I took off my raincoat and plugged in the kettle. I heard "Next!" and presuming he meant me, I walked to the table and flipped over the page to the next picture. A delicate-winged faery, hovering over a bluebell, stared back at us. The leprechaun pointed to the faery and it became three-dimensional and started to move. The little 'uns were captivated, and the smallest one leaned forward and poked the faery in the tummy. The little faery, caught off guard, quickly retaliated. Bending over with the speed of light, it bit the offending finger. The little leprechaun let out a howl and, sobbing, disappeared into the void. His older brother quickly followed.

"Children," my friend muttered, throwing up his hands in mock despair. Hearing the kettle boil, I gestured for him to sit on the couch and went to make the tea.

Returning with two steaming mugs, I sat down beside him. Studying me closely, he commented, "You've met your body elemental."

"How did you know?" I laughed. As usual, he had anticipated my news.

"It's written all over you," he replied, sipping his tea languidly.

"Come on, come on, more detail," I probed, delighted. It was such a pleasure to see him again. I had missed our morning chats.

"It's not that easy to explain to a human," he said, puffing himself up to indicate his superiority in this seemingly complex area. Smiling inwardly at his now familiar habit of suspenseful story-telling, with eyes downcast, I said in a pleading voice, "Please proceed as best you can. This poor simple human would greatly appreciate it."

"You've upped me again," he shrieked, collapsing in laughter on the couch. "You're getting too good."

Pulling himself together, he continued more seriously. "Before, when I looked at you, I saw two beings—you and your body elemental. They were separate, as is the case in most humans."

"And now?" I asked, coaxing him along.

"Now they're more together, but 'together' is not exactly the right word," he said stroking his chin and searching for a more precise definition. "It's as if your body elemental was caged inside you and now it's free and is moving through all your cells. It has expanded its territory."

In my mind I saw an image of a wispy, amorphous amoeba moving through my body, continually shrinking and stretching. Sometimes it was the size of my entire body and overlaid me. Other times it was concentrated in a certain part of my body. When it overlaid me, it looked almost human, as if it were looking through my eyes. I projected these images to the leprechaun for confirmation.

"That's what it looks like to you," he both confirmed and corrected me. "To me, your body elemental is a sparkling life force that permeates your body. Did you know that when you die it usually takes three days for the body elemental to totally extricate itself from your body?"

"That's why so many religions don't bury their dead for three days and that's why Jesus rose from the dead after three days, isn't it?" I asked, feeling ideas click into place.

"Correct," he said.

"Do you have a body elemental like humans?" I asked, surprised that I already knew the answer.

"No, we don't," said the leprechaun and I could feel a deep reluctance in him to speak.

Unwilling to let the matter drop, I continued, "I need to know why!"

"Of course you do," he smiled sadly, before continuing on a happier note. "Our discussion has branched into an area of deep secrets for elementals and I'm beyond what I can teach you. I've spent the last few days with my teachers and have permission to bring you to them for further instruction."

Looking down at my flannel nightie, I protested quickly, "Not yet. I've got to get dressed first."

"It's really not necessary," he laughed. "You can be dressed any way you want in my world. Now close your eyes."

Doing as he instructed, I felt a black tunnel open around me. Within a millisecond, I was standing in a meadow of wildflowers, surrounded by gigantic old oaks and hawthorn. The leprechaun stood beside me, dressed in a glistening white robe with a shamrock covering his heart like a shield. Perched on his head was his ever-present top hat. Looking down at myself, I found that I wore a similar robe with a bright red rose emblazoned across my heart.

"I took the liberty of dressing you for the occasion," he said, striding purposefully towards the oak grove. I hastened to keep up.

Walking among the tall oaks, I observed carpets of bluebells covering the forest floor. The light shimmered in the leaves, creating an aura of mystery. The air was filled with voices whispering, "Who is she? Who is she?" and then a silence fell. Looking up, I saw an ancient, white-bearded elemental watching our approach. He, too, was dressed in a long white robe and there was a flame insignia across his chest. In his right hand he held a long walking cane, taller than him, and on his head rested a conical hat. A wizard, was the thought that came to mind.

"Welcome to our land," he greeted me, as we came within earshot. His eyes radiated old power and secrets. "Our young friend has been teaching you very well about elementals, but there are things that he is still learning so we thought it best to teach both of you at the same time."

He pointed his walking stick towards a gigantic oak tree, and its three gnarled roots immediately extended themselves to form indentations like chairs. The old elemental walked forward and sat down, signaling us to do the same. My leprechaun friend seemed to have forgotten to make introductions and was strangely silent. Following his example, I waited for the old one to speak.

"You're here to learn more about body elementals," he commenced without pleasantries. "I understand our young friend told you that we don't have body elementals. Why do you think that is?"

I was so used to the leprechaun answering my questions that I was caught off guard. The old one waited patiently for my answer.

Searching my memories, I found nothing. I did the only thing I could think of under the circumstances. I stretched my consciousness into the body of my host and looked to see if I could find the answer there. What I found was an energy source so vast that all cells vibrated with a multitude of colors and sounds. Yet amidst it all there was only one consciousness—his.

Withdrawing, I was surprised to see him smiling at my leprechaun friend and saying in mock sympathy, "She's been a handful for you, hasn't she?"

"Why would I take something on speculation without checking it myself?" I said, defending myself. "I can't find a body elemental inside you, like I seem to have, but I don't know the reason so I'd be pleased if you would tell me."

"When you were inside me, what did you comprehend?" the old one asked.

"I saw your cells alive with energy and controlled by your consciousness," I replied, reliving the experience.

"And did you see my soul?" he asked.

"To be frank, I've always been confused about the difference between soul and spirit," I replied. "With humans, I can see their previous lives and the purpose of their present life and know if they are on or off track. What I think of as their soul's purpose is just the higher aspect of who they are. And spirit? Well, I think of the holy spirit as a spark of life, a divine fire that the creator gave to each of us to help us live in accordance with the overall divine plan."

Pulling on his beard, he considered my words and asked, "And would you say that I have a soul and a spirit?"

"As I said," I responded, "I don't know that I'm qualified to judge. I have trouble with this question even with humans, let alone with elementals."

"I'm asking for your judgment," pressed the old one. I could see that I wasn't going to get any answers that I couldn't work out for myself.

Concentrating on his question, I reentered his body and once again was surrounded by the incredible life force of him. As I had experienced before, I could feel that his energy flowed in accordance with the divine spirit, but I couldn't find anything resembling a soul.

"So?" he asked, arching his eyebrow just like my leprechaun friend did.

"All spirit, no soul, would be my guess," I replied.

"Correct," he replied. "Now enter our young friend."

Turning to my leprechaun friend, I mentally asked permission and was given it. Entering his body, I could see immediately that he didn't have nearly the life force of the old one. There also seemed to be a denseness in him that was not in his teacher. In order to fully understand, I looked closer and my immediate thought was that he felt more like me. He was more solid. Confused, I withdrew and shared my observations with them.

"What you are seeing," the old one commented, "is the beginnings of a body elemental. Our young friend decided long ago to work with humans to become a creator and his body is changing from a purely elemental form to become denser like yours. To keep his memories, he is working with his own body elemental so that he will be able to die and still remember his previous incarnations. In the elemental world, we can live a long time—almost a thousand years, as I have done—but when we die our energy is given back to the Earth and we have no memory to carry forward into another life. To have this memory, we would need a body elemental."

I was astounded by this information and now understood why he had prompted me to reach these conclusions by myself. I might not have believed his words.

"Humans sacrifice their communion with the divine spirit in order to evolve into creators, don't they?" I asked, sharing an insight about my own race.

"Yes, they do," he replied, "but ultimately you become as much divine fire as I am, and with a memory that goes from life to life. You become both spirit and what you humans call soul."

"Is soul another word for the body elemental?" I asked, still intrigued.

"It is," said he. "Even animals in your world are part of a group soul but they don't individualize. Elementals, like animals, have group souls. There's a group soul for each kind of elemental, including faeries, devas, gnomes, goblins, sylphs, sprites, and even leprechauns. Just as animals, such as cats, have different personalities but are still cats, we too have different personalities but are much more tied to our group soul than are humans."

It was at that moment that my leprechaun friend finally decided to speak. "The new caste that was formed almost a hundred years ago is comprised of elementals from all different castes so that we can learn diversity from each other. That will help each of us to individuate. All members of our group are hosts to body elementals and, as such, are mutants in our world. We are regarded as thick and dense by other elementals and there may come a time when it is harder for us to stay here than to go to your human world."

"Except," the old one interrupted, correcting my friend, "many humans are engaged in altering the vibration of their world now. When humans plant more trees than they cut down, kill only what they need to eat, and work in accordance with the divine plan, they lighten the vibration in their world, bringing it closer to ours. Before too many years have passed, both our worlds will start overlapping as they did long ago." As he spoke, a look of longing crossed his face.

"Did you ever enter my world?" I asked politely.

"In my youth, many hundreds of years ago," he spoke wistfully, "humans and elementals were more alike. Both worlds were covered with lush forest, meadows, clean streams, and lakes. Humans don't understand the importance that their physical environment has on their spirit. You were lighter and cleaner when you lived close to nature. You had less knowledge but more wisdom then. When your spirits and bodies were cleaner, you could often see elementals. You gave us gifts of food and celebrations at the turning of the seasons to thank us for our help in growing your crops. Your recognition of us strengthened our presence in your world."

"And you think we will work and play together again?" I asked the old one hopefully.

"It's recorded so," he responded. Looking at my leprechaun friend and back to me, I could feel him weaving our energies closer together.

"There are many humans," the old one said, "working to cleanse the world of pollution and greed, and there are many elementals working to become creators to maintain the Earth."

"Why do you not have a body elemental like our young friend?" I said, goading my leprechaun friend with the old one's title.

"The choice to become a creator was not available when I was young," the old one responded. "When the choice was offered, it was too late for me to change. Still, I can work with young elementals—like our young friend here—to pass on my wisdom, and they will remember it for me. And sometimes I can work with humans like you if their spirit is both light and strong enough for me to bear their presence and they to bear mine."

I could feel that our discussion was ending, but was dying to know if he was a leprechaun or some other kind of elemental, and what his talents were. I was just on the point of asking when he said,

"We'll talk about other species of elementals tomorrow. It's time that you returned home and got dressed."

I looked down and was horrified to see myself once again clothed in my granny gown. Both the old one and my leprechaun friend dissolved into laughter and I found myself back in the bedroom standing before my unmade bed.

CHAPTER SEVENTEEN

Earth, Air, Fire, and Water

 WAITED EAGERLY FOR THE NEXT DAY, several questions pressed on my mind. The morning dawned in a blaze of sun and I carried two chairs and two cups of tea outside and sat down. I was soaking up the sun's rays and breathing in the cool, fresh air when the leprechaun materialized in the other chair.

"Good mornin' to ya," he greeted me, tipping his hat. "You made quite an impression on the old one. I can't understand why, but he'd like to see you again today."

"I'd be most happy to see him again, young one," I teased, keen to make up for the nightgown incident.

"That's enough of that," he reprimanded, pretending he was upset, "or I'll not take you."

"Okay, truce," I said, happy to be bargaining with all my clothes on.

"Truce," he returned and, pointing his finger behind me, opened a black tunnel that swallowed me up. In the blink of an eye, we were sitting on the same gnarled oak tree, right beside the old one.

"I've been giving some thought to the different insignias on your chests," I said, in true elemental fashion, as if no time had passed.

"And?" the old one questioned, awaiting my conclusion. He was pleased to see that I now understood his system of me telling him the answers, rather than the other way around.

"Your insignias have to do with your soul talent," I said. Then remembering that he had no soul, I corrected myself, "I mean the essence of your being."

Smiling, he replied, "That's correct. So what do our insignias represent?"

Looking at the flame on his chest, I replied, "You burn with the divine fire of the creator."

He nodded approval. Pointing to the rose on my chest, He asked, "And you?"

I continued, "The rose is the mystical symbol of enlightenment for the West, just like the lotus is for the East. In the human mystical tradition there are twelve rays of power that create our world, and to become a creator each of us must learn to use the gifts of each of these rays. Five of these rays are unmanifested, meaning that their gift is to dissolve or eliminate what is no longer needed in the world. The rose is one of the five unmanifested rays. My gift is to help people to eliminate or demanifest what is not needed in their lives, be it in their thoughts, feelings, or relationships. That's why my insignia is a rose."

"Not bad," the old one replied, "and what about the shamrock on our young friend?"

"Other than the fact that he's Irish and the shamrock is associated with Ireland, I don't know," I answered, hoping he wouldn't make me try to work it out.

Turning to my leprechaun friend, the old one waited for his response.

"A shamrock has got four petals, indicating our control of the four main elements in nature—earth, air, fire, and water. All elementals who work in our caste have this insignia," he replied, looking from me to the old one.

"Next question?" the old one commanded, wasting no time.

"To which species of elemental evolution do you belong?" I asked, not wanting to appear rude, but trying to understand. He looked fairly human, though smaller and with eyes slanted in a typically elemental way. I was confused.

"Your problem is that your preconceived view denies the truth of your perception," the old one shot back.

I knew I was good at simplifying the complex, but was less expert at seeing what was obvious to others. Deciding to focus my attention on the obvious, I looked at his insignia.

"You're a fire elemental?" I asked, still not fully trusting my own perception.

"That's right," the old one answered, smiling. "I've taken a form with which you'd have more comfort. But you should have paid more attention to your own observation when you encountered my true internal essence."

I struggled to remember what I knew of fire elementals, which was basically that they flicked through the flames in the fireplace. Undines, were they called? No, that was water elementals. Sylphs? No, that was air. I couldn't remember their name but, whatever the case, this old one did not look anything like what I'd thought of as fire elementals.

"You're stuck in your prejudices again," the old one said, reading my mind, "and the word you're looking for is salamander. Your image of salamanders stems from the very beginning of our evolution. Gradually, as we evolve, we carry more and more of the creator's fire."

"That doesn't happen in just one of your lives, does it?" I asked.

"No. To become a master takes us as many lives as for humans," he replied, and continued, "Fire is the highest of the elements. You have fire in your body that humans call *kundalini* energy. This kundalini energy carries the divine life force of the Creator through a central energy channel that runs up your spinal cord. This channel is connected to the seven major energy centers in your body that you call *chakras.* The kundalini fire nourishes these chakras which in turn energize all your organs to which the chakras are connected. Even your blood carries the life force of fire energy. Fire is needed to manifest what you want in both of our worlds. It is the spark that triggers every manifestation."

As he spoke, I thought of the mental fire-lighting exercise I had been practicing all summer. I'd been unsuccessful, despite my numerous arduous attempts.

"It's because you don't really believe that you can light the fire with your mind. Your lack of belief cancels your thought of doing it," the old one stated, casually lighting the end of his staff so that it glowed like a torch. Feeling something swell in my hand, I glanced down and found it contained a similar staff.

"Now, you try," he commanded.

Allowing my consciousness to enter my body, I hooked my attention into my root chakra, which is the seat of my fire energy that is connected to the energy of the Earth. Pulling the fire up through my body, I imagined that the end of my staff was on fire. The fire blazed. Shocked, I shut down my mind in disbelief and the flame went out. Trying again, I imagined that a flame from the old one's staff jumped over and lit mine. It worked for a few seconds until he snuffed it out.

"That's not allowed," he scolded, smiling. "You'll never learn to do it yourself if you do not believe in yourself. Start again."

I realized that I was afraid of my own fire. For several years, I had spontaneous burns and blisters on my hands and body, and had even been taken to the hospital for them. They'd been diagnosed as second degree burns, but no reason for them could be found. The only thing that had soothed my skin was baths for a week or two until the fire had subsided. I was always surprised when my body totally healed without scarring.

"These burns are the result of you carrying too much fire without grounding and channeling it back into the world," the old one said encouragingly. "You must learn to release the fire into the world and the burns will pass. It is not by accident that I have been assigned to teach you. Control of all four elements must be mastered in order to be a well-balanced creator who can create a world. This is what the being who created this planet, the one you call God, has done. But fire is the most important element, as it is needed to create things quickly in your third-dimensional world. Now try again."

Returning my attention to my inner fire, I allowed it to rise through me once again until I felt as if my entire body were on fire. I hoped there was a water elemental around in case this experiment got out of hand. My fire kept dying down and then flaring up. I had little control over it. I decided to create something positive with the fire and immediately an image of a cozy fire in my hearth came to mind. Opening my eyes, I saw my hearth standing in the forest with a wonderful fire blazing in it.

"This is the fire that you have been creating every day with your concentration," the old one observed. "It manifests much easier in our world than in yours, which is so heavy and dense. You have created the fire in the ether, which holds the memory of all your thoughts. So don't despair that you have failed."

At this moment my leprechaun friend, who had been silently following our conversation, interrupted, "It might be a good time to introduce her to some of the others."

"Indeed, it would," replied the old one. "Let's see if Water can come."

A moment later another chair appeared in the roots of the tree and a second elemental, identical to the old one, sat there. A slow smile came to his face. Bowing, the fire elemental disappeared and his chair reabsorbed itself into the tree.

Turning towards the water elemental, I noticed immediately that an insignia of a deep blue standing wave moved across his chest. His eyes were very different from those of the fire elemental. Whereas the latter's eyes glowed and sparkled with the fire that lay behind them, this elemental's eyes held the peace of a deep blue sea. I felt as calmed by his presence as I had been stimulated by the other's.

"Water's just what I need," I said, taking a deep breath and sinking into the peace of his aura. My leprechaun friend coughed to get my attention and, shaking his head, motioned for me to shut up. Different rules again, I thought, closing my mouth.

"What do you think of our world so far?" asked the water elemental politely.

"I am enjoying myself very much," I said courteously, wondering if circuitous approaches were typical of his element. I settled deeper into his peace and felt myself caring less and less whether we spoke or not.

"That's what happens when humans have too much water," he said, rousing me from my reverie. "They become lazy, unformed, and indecisive."

Eager to prove that I could still think, I pulled myself away from the sinking peace and asked, "And what is the correct amount of water for a human?"

"When you are balanced between the being state of water and the doing state of fire, you are in correct proportion," the water elemental replied.

Out of the corner of my eye, I caught a glimpse of my leprechaun friend. He seemed amazed that the water elemental was speaking.

"I can still speak," said the old one to him gently. "It's just that I prefer not to when I teach you and, if I had longer with your human friend, I'd not talk to her either."

Turning to me, the water elemental continued, "As you can see, my gift is one of peace and tranquillity, of being, not doing."

"Although I feel peaceful with you," I said, "bubbling brooks, raging rivers, and stormy oceans don't have the peace of which you speak."

"Oh that," he answered, smiling languidly, "is not the true essence of water. That is water stirred up by fire or air. Water is the base element of this planet and, as you know, much of your body is water. Water is the conductor through which the elements of fire, air, and earth move in your body."

Looking at me, he continued, "Water lubricates your body so that it can move. It is the juice in your mouth that allows you to taste. Have you never thought of the water of the unconscious that holds the potential to bring dreams into reality?"

As the water elemental spoke, I was reminded of how much I loved to swim in lakes and oceans in the summer. Doing this, I felt restored to something of primal importance, devoid of any intellectual thought. Also, I recalled some of my best insights occurred while meditating in the shower. Yet overall, I thought I understood fire and air better than water.

The water elemental interrupted my thoughts and stated, "All beings have specific elements with which they are more in harmony but, as the fire elemental must have told you, control and knowledge of all four elements are necessary in order to become a creator. Keep swimming."

He finished speaking and another being, identical to the other two except for an empty space on his chest, appeared beside him. The water elemental continued to sit there, calmly observing. Not wishing to offend, I said nothing. This was probably not the correct approach as this new elemental, more diaphanous than the other two, was threatening to disappear altogether.

"You must be Air," I said, calling it into form with my question.

"Right," it chirped happily, continuing to drift in and out of form on the chair.

"Can you hold a form like the fire and water elementals?" I asked.

"Of course I can, if I borrow some of the earth element," it commented and immediately solidified. "I thought that I'd show you more of my true form so you could understand me better."

"Would it help if I entered you as I entered Fire?" I asked curiously.

"Go ahead," it invited, waiting for me to commence.

I directed my consciousness inside the air elemental. Surprised, I saw nothing there but space and ether. Looking around for the consciousness of the air elemental, I found it watching and listening to me wherever I looked. I withdrew and tried to make sense of the experience.

"Are you the space between all matter?" I asked, believing I'd found the right interpretation.

"That I am," he said. "Your human scientists are only now discovering how much space exists in matter, and I'm that space. By controlling my element, both humans and elementals can travel in space, time, and between dimensions. I prefer to think of myself as space or ether, rather than air. Air is just a bi-product of my essence."

As he spoke, I took a closer look at his chest, trying to locate his insignia. What I saw instead were subtle, barely-visible currents of swirling energy. His eyes were different also. They were bottomless pits of empty space into which I could fall, if I did not hold my attention where I was.

"Our young friend," the air elemental said, nodding towards the leprechaun, "uses my element to bring you to us and can take you on journeys to other places."

Before I could thank him for his information, the air elemental disappeared and another much more solid elemental replaced him. Once again, this one looked identical to the others except for a multicolored crystal insignia across his breast. He appeared more gnarled than the others and his eyes kept changing color, from green to brown. He was obviously the elemental for Earth.

"You've met the other three so you might as well meet me," he growled towards me.

I was wondering why he was antagonistic and he answered my thought.

"You humans are killing the world," he said accusingly.

"I can understand your anger but I am not doing this personally and am, in fact, trying to do positive things to help the world," I retorted, defending myself.

"You are not doing half as much as you could be doing," the earth elemental countered.

Our relationship was disintegrating before it even started, so I decided on a different approach. "You are probably right," I said, "but I've had a long morning and I think we could accomplish a great deal more for the world if we tried again tomorrow. Would that be acceptable to you?"

I could feel waves of soothing calm emanating from the water elemental who had been watching our exchange. Turning his head to acknowledge some unspoken message from his fellow elemental, the earth elemental turned back to me and said in a subdued but still grudging manner, "I accept your suggestion and will see you here tomorrow."

The tunnel appeared in front of me and I was returned to my chair in the garden. The sun, which had been rising when I left, had now passed its zenith in the sky. Two half-empty cups of cold tea sat on the ground beside the chairs. Exhausted, I picked up the cups, took them back to the kitchen, and lay down on the couch for a nap. I was shaken by my confrontation with the earth elemental and was not looking forward to the next day. I realized, however, that I had to go. I felt like I was being accused of crimes committed by all humanity and that somehow I had to defend my race. I grimaced at the irony of my situation. I myself was usually the accuser when I saw what other humans were doing to the Earth.

CHAPTER EIGHTEEN

Crimes Against the Earth

EXT MORNING I WAS BOILING THE WATER FOR TEA, hoping to soothe away the feeling of cold dread in the pit of my stomach. Where was my leprechaun friend when I needed him, I wondered, sending out a mental call for help.

"I'm here," he said, materializing beside me in a long black gown—the kind worn by judges and choir singers. It took no great wisdom to figure out which role he was playing today.

"Oh no," I groaned, unplugging the boiling kettle. "I don't think I'll go. Couldn't we just sit in the garden and meet flower faeries?"

"Another day," he said sternly. "Now make the tea and we'll have a talk before leaving."

I put one more tea bag than usual in the pot. Maybe extra caffeine would help, I thought halfheartedly. Wandering to the bathroom, I brushed my teeth vigorously and rinsed my face with cold water. Returning to the bedroom, I pulled on my wool sweater and thought how nice it would be to go south for a week in the sun. Returning to the kitchen, I lifted the tea pot and two cups and walked outside. My leprechaun friend was already seated in his chair, waiting.

Sighing, I sank into my chair. I closed my eyes, hoping that I could blink away today and move to tomorrow.

I remembered once hearing that the best line of defense was taking the offense, so I said, "It's not fair that I'm being blamed for all of humanity and what it's done to the Earth."

No response from the leprechaun.

"I'm prepared to take punishment for my own actions," I said. "Now that's fair, isn't it?"

The leprechaun continued to sit in silence, refusing to be drawn into debate.

"After all, I'm a guest in your realm. Is this any way to treat a guest?" I asked rhetorically, upping the ante.

Realizing that I was getting absolutely nowhere, I sighed, poured the tea and, capitulating, said, "When do we go?"

"Just as soon as we have our tea," he replied, holding his etheric cup in two hands and raising it to his puckered lips.

Sitting in silence, I ran through the possible worst case scenarios, but most of them had the same basic theme—human disappears from remote Irish cottage and is never seen again.

Trying to engage the leprechaun in conversation one more time, I asked, "Can't you give me any idea of how to handle this?"

"Sorry, not allowed," he replied, setting down his empty cup and glancing into mine, which was almost full. I had been trying to put off the inevitable as long as possible.

Resigned, I downed the tea and said as bravely as I could manage, "Ready." As we disappeared into the tunnel, my leprechaun friend winked at me encouragingly.

I found myself standing in the oak grove, but much had changed. Instead of the white robe, I was clothed in a kind of sackcloth from which hung dead leaves and disturbing images—birds poisoned by insecticides, dead animals with men standing over them with guns, entire forests devastated with nothing left but blackened stumps.

In place of the peace that I had associated with this grove, I felt anger everywhere. Ahead of me stood the four elementals of earth, air, fire, and water, dressed as before, but their eyes were no longer the same. I could see the raw power of storms, volcanoes, torna-does, and earthquakes in them and was terrified of that energy being directed at me.

"Today you are to stand trial," began the fire elemental, "for crimes against the Earth. How do you plead?"

"Guilty," I replied. What defense could I offer for what fellow humans and I had done?

"Do you have anything to say in your defense?" asked the water elemental.

Thinking deeper, I answered, "Ignorance."

"State your case," replied the air elemental, sweeping the dead leaves off my robe in a sudden gust of air.

"Humans are children, baby creators," I said, defending hu-manity. "We cannot be judged as fully-functioning adults who do responsible things. Unlike elementals, we have lost touch with the divine spirit, which guides you in your positive work for the Earth. Without this internal guidance, we are struggling through trial and error to rediscover the right laws. Like children who crave candy until they get sick, we have eaten up the resources of the Earth and are now suffering the effects."

The elementals listened without comment, so I continued, "Humans, like elementals, cannot be judged as a race. Individuals in both of our races are at various stages in their evolution. I will not deny that the world is still full of greedy humans who feed their own egotistical needs, but a change has occurred in the last forty years. That's a very short amount of time—even smaller in your lifetime—so maybe you don't notice it, but more and more humans are working to preserve nature. We have started replanting forests that we killed. We are eliminating the hunting of animals for sport. We are healing with the crystals of the mineral world and talking to plants. We eat foods lower down on the food chain."

They were still listening in silence, so I went on, "I'm not saying that we don't still have much further to go. But humans are attempting to become more responsible, and we could use your help."

I looked down at my robe and noticed that it had started to change. The dead leaves now showed tinges of green. The dead forests had small trees and flowers growing between the stumps. There were eagles sitting on a nest that held two eggs, and people were shooting elephants in Africa with cameras instead of guns.

Filling with hope, I looked up and saw all four examining me. I suddenly knew that I was in the presence of four masters of the elemental world. Because I was human, the direction of my evolution did not come under their auspices, but I now understood that I had been sent to work with them as a bridge between our two worlds. Their testing of me was a kind of initiation, similar to the initiation I was undergoing that summer in the human world. They were testing my resolve to serve the world and all beings.

Allowing these observations to sink in, they remained quiet. Finally, the earth elemental, who had been so antagonistic the previous day, turned to my leprechaun friend and asked, "What is your judgment?"

So absorbed had I been with the process, that I had completely forgotten my friend's presence. Looking to my right, I saw him, still dressed in his black robe, sitting behind a large desk with a gavel in his hand.

Lifting it up and striking the table, he pronounced, "Not guilty by reason of ignorance," he replied and, staring at me, continued, "However she is not totally absolved. I recommend a penance."

"And what would that be?" the earth elemental said, agreeing to the judgment.

"She must write a book about our world and elemental evolution so that humans can no longer plead ignorance and will, instead, work with us consciously to heal the Earth," he replied adamantly.

"Agreed," all four elementals said jointly.

The earth elemental turned to me and continued, "This book will not be written now, for the time is not yet right. It will be written in ten years' time. Meanwhile, you will prepare people's minds and hearts so that they will welcome our message. You will also assist others who are working with us either consciously or unconsciously."

"I agree," I replied and, as I watched, the four turned to me with their staffs and shot a bolt of energy into my body. I was knocked unconscious by the shock and some hours later came to, sitting in my chair in the garden.

CHAPTER NINETEEN

Working Together

SITTING IN THE GARDEN AFTER DINNER THAT EVENING, I was thinking about my experience when unexpectedly the leprechaun appeared. No longer dressed in the black robe, he wore his usual long-sleeved green waistcoat, brown trousers, and ever-present black top hat.

"I didn't expect you until tomorrow," I said, greeting him.

"Couldn't wait, couldn't wait, so much to do," he muttered in a dither.

I had become so used to his scholarly persona that to see him flustered like the Mad Hatter in *Alice in Wonderland* was disconcerting. I got up to prepare him a calming cup of tea when he grabbed my arm and pushed me back into my chair.

"No time, no time," he continued, still in a frenzy.

"Tell me what has happened," I asked him in my most reassuring voice.

"I've been given the responsibility," he whispered and stopped. He was withholding some important secret.

"Of what?" I asked, eager to get the whole story.

"Of the book and seeing that you get all the right information and finding all the right elementals to work with us and everything, just everything," he replied, taking off his hat and mopping his brow. For once he didn't seem to be acting.

Sympathizing, I asked, "What happened after I left?"

"I'd better start from the beginning," he said, looking at me in kindly exasperation, as if explaining something to a child. "I know that you humans, locked in time as you are, always have to start at the beginning in order to understand." Putting his hat back on his head and relaxing into his chair, he commenced, "I was looking forward to you coming to live here, just as much as you were looking forward to being enlightened." He spoke the last word with his nose in the air and in a fake upper class British voice. I was glad to see that his humor had returned.

"As I told you before," he continued, "I'm preparing for the same initiations in my world as you are in yours, and learning more about humans from you and teaching you is all part of my study.

"But," he paused, "they've just changed the rules. I've got to work with you for years and years, and I've got to make sure you write this book and get all the right information." He wrung his hands in distress as he spoke.

"Well, the rules were changed on me as well," I said, commiserating with him. "Remember, I thought that I'd meditate all summer and become enlightened. Instead, I'm living in a haunted cottage, taking trips to your world to defend humans, and now I find out that, not only do I not become enlightened, but I must also write a book about this entire experience in ten years' time. Has it occurred to anyone to wonder how I'm going to remember all this, a decade from now?"

"Oh, don't worry about remembering, because I'll be there to help you," he said, waving his hand dismissively. "You know," he said, changing the subject, "they're doing this to make me become a creator more quickly. But they're not going to help, they're just going to watch to see how I do." As he spoke, another wave of anxiety washed over him at the prospect of having to become a creator without help.

"Oh, don't worry about that," I reassured him. "Humans go through their whole lives acting on their own. I'll help you with that."

We looked at each other and started to laugh. We had both just realized that my weakness was his strength, and vice versa. Obviously it was no accident that we'd been thrown together.

I was the first to speak. "Those four elementals are your teachers, aren't they?" I asked and then, as an afterthought, added, "And they don't really look like that, do they?"

"Yes, they're my teachers, but what did they look like to you?" he asked, puzzled by my question.

"They all looked identical—white hair and beards, tall wizard hat, white robe, you know?" I replied, confused by his question.

He started to laugh again and replied, "That's not at all how they look to me. Senior elementals can take any form they wish but only masters can create different forms for different beings to see at the same time. They took a form with which you'd feel comfortable."

"What did they look like to you?" I asked, intrigued.

Recalling our two trips together, he struggled to find words that I could understand. "Earth, Ether, Fire, and Water continually change their form to become what they speak of. Sometimes they look like an elemental that is associated with each element—such as Earth taking the shape of a gnome. Sometimes they look like a standing wave or a crystal or a whirlwind."

As he spoke, I was reminded of the forms emblazoned on their chests and realized that they were miniature images of the entire being that my leprechaun friend saw.

Curious, I asked, "How do they teach you?" I was quite sure that they didn't just talk, as human teachers most often do.

"Our elemental masters enter our bodies so that we fully experience who they are. This way we become like them," he replied, adding sadly, "but that's happening less and less now.

"Because our group is becoming denser, more human, it's more difficult for them to enter and change us," he continued. "Instead, they're talking to us more now and we practice what they're saying. It's very difficult for elementals to learn in this manner. But that's the way that humans do it and that's the way I've been communicating with you. I'll probably be sent to some of your human masters—just like you were sent to my elemental masters—so that I can learn more about human evolution."

"Do you enter other elementals when you teach them?" I asked.

"Sometimes, with their permission, except that I'm not teaching all elementals," the leprechaun replied. "I'm just teaching those in our caste who want to work with humans. To do this, I extend my body elemental into the body of my student so that he can experience what I'm saying. It's the same as you did with the masters. We also talk a lot in our caste because it's difficult, with so many kinds of elementals, for us to be inside each other's bodies for a long time. We will be able to do this more when we become stronger and less likely to lose our own identity.

"But," he said, "this is not the way that most elementals learn. Most enter the other being because their goal is to become the same kind of elemental. Our caste is the exception."

I could not remember him ever entering my body and was curious to know if that would help him in some way.

"No, it wouldn't," he replied, catching my thought. "It's too dangerous. Your ego is too strong for me and I'd be imprinted to be like you. It's much better if we learn through talking, because even when you talk, your essence floods over me. It's all I can take."

"But you gave me permission to enter you when we were with the fire elemental," I asked, not understanding. "What was the difference?"

"We were in the elemental world and your ego was much weaker and of no danger to me," he replied. "Here, in your world, you are much stronger than me."

"Is there anything you would like to change about the way we spend time together?" I asked, anxious to maximize our learning.

"No," he smiled, catching my thought, "I'm happy with our progress."

During our talk, he had relaxed more and more and was no longer anxious about what his teachers had asked of him. Believing that it was time to bring him back to that topic, I said, "So we agree that we are working well together and have both learned a great deal. But now we must think of how best to help elementals and humans to work together. That's our purpose, after all."

He waited for me to continue. We seemed to have broken new ground, with humans having the advantage.

"Your caste of elementals is committed to working with humans for two reasons: so that they can become creators and to help our planet. Do each of these elementals have a human with whom to work?" I probed for more information.

"Unfortunately not," he replied. "For a couple of reasons. First, there are not enough humans like you who are interested or who can directly access the elemental realms. Second, there are not enough elementals strong enough to hold themselves in the human world as I am doing."

"The elemental masters said that in ten years humans will be more interested in working with elementals," I interjected. "Will the elementals in your caste be strong enough to work with these humans by then?"

"The older ones, who joined when I did, could do so now," he replied, stroking his chin thoughtfully. If we focus on helping the newer ones to build a more solid ego, they will be ready in ten years. We should talk about how humans can cooperate with elementals to help the planet."

"I'm all ears," I said, imagining that I'd grown gigantic elfin ears.

Looking at me, he dissolved into laughter. "Do you know that you actually grow ears in the etheric plane when you visualize them?" he asked, knowing full well that I hadn't thought of that.

I instinctively reached up to check the size of my ears.

"They don't grow in physical reality, only etheric reality," said my leprechaun friend, shaking his head at my ignorance.

"Humans have no idea that every thought they think makes a record in the ethers. The stronger the thought, the stronger the record," he said, teaching me the basics. "If humans imagined clean water and healthy forests and called on the elementals of these places to help, they could restore health to this planet in no time."

"That's a wonderful thought," I said. "However, how can this happen if people continue depleting our wildlife and cutting down old growth forests?"

"You're right, of course," the leprechaun responded. "Both changes must happen simultaneously."

"That's why it feels so hopeless," I said despondently. "How can one person meditating and talking to elementals negate the effect of thousands of people who are bent on raping the lands and oceans?"

"One person working with the divine will affects thousands of people who are not. As you yourself said to the masters, humans are changing. We must visualize the way they are becoming and not collapse into the old image of what they have been."

I was amused at his defense of humans and asked in all seriousness, "Have you got any ideas of how humans can work most effectively with elementals?"

"Lots of them," he replied, obviously bursting to be asked. "I've written something for the occasion, which I call:

Ten Ways for Humans to Work with Elementals

1. Believe in elementals. Human belief strengthens elementals and gives them energy.
2. Be happy and enthusiastic. Elementals are not attracted to depressed, sad humans.
3. Go to healthy places in nature as often as possible. Walk in forests, along the seashore, lie in a meadow, listen to birds, sit by a brook. Enter into the right vibration of the Earth and listen

to what it wants. Humans will purify their vibrations if they do these things.

4. Appreciate the beauty in nature. When humans do this, elementals will be attracted to you.

5. Cooperate and create with nature by planting trees, growing flowers, feeding the birds.

6. Send energy to elementals who look after trees, flowers, water, and mountains, to keep them healthy. Do this with joy and gratitude.

7. Teach other humans to appreciate nature. Do it with love and joy, and these humans will begin to understand the Earth's needs.

8. Do things spontaneously; free yourself from overplanning and organizing.

9. Take time every day to do nothing. Create a space in both your house and head so magic can occur.

10. In order to contact an elemental who wants to work with you on an ongoing basis, sit in a quiet natural place, close your eyes, and call this elemental to you. Notice what kind of elemental has come. Ask it what its gift is and its name. Listen to this elemental on an ongoing basis; act on its suggestions, and your relationship will become stronger."

"They're wonderful," I said, congratulating him. "But your suggestions are more focused on what humans can do. Let's see if I can think of recommendations for what elementals can do." I pondered for several minutes, then continued, "Let's call it:

Ten Ways for Elementals to Work with Humans

1. Do not prejudge all humans as bad but examine each human to find the good in them.

2. Having found the spark of good, breathe your energy into it to enlarge it.

3. When a human pays attention to a plant, tree, or stone, tell him or her what the plant or tree would like in order to be healthier. Even if humans don't hear the message consciously, they will receive it subconsciously.

4. When you see a human who is trying to help nature, cluster around that human and give them all the help you can. Often humans don't think to ask you directly, but our higher selves ask this.

5. Play with humans so that they can recover their childlike joy and wonder. Many humans are depressed and need the joy elementals bring.

6. Give humans proof of your existence. Humans are more inclined to believe in elementals if you do this.

7. Appreciate human strengths of forgiveness, love, persistence, and focus. By associating with humans, elementals will learn these qualities.

8. To body elementals: don't give up. Keep moving your human hosts into situations to catalyze positive change.

9. Don't judge humans by elemental standards. Presently, humans eat beings that live, excrete waste, and age. Through this path we learn to be creators of form and worlds.

10. Surprise us."

"Very good indeed," the leprechaun said. "I think we've made an excellent start for today. I'll see you tomorrow, and prepare yourself to receive a guest."

What does he mean by "guest?" I was left wondering as he disappeared.

CHAPTER TWENTY

Being from the Center of the Earth

OST EVENINGS FOUND ME SITTING IN BED doing my nightly meditation by candlelight. In the absence of the leprechauns and Mrs. O'Toole, a thick silence often descended on the cottage at night. The one ceiling fixture in the living room was not good enough to read by and in any event I had nothing but the Bible to read. So often around nine-thirty or ten o'clock, I headed for bed to start my evening practice.

Filling up the hot water bottles, I'd place them strategically under the covers, warming the spots where my feet and bum would soon be. Then, throwing off my clothes, I'd pull on my granny gown, topped by my wool sweater, and jump in. On a table beside the bed was a small bedside lamp. Beside it sat the Bible that my parents had given me at confirmation. It contained lovely colored pictures of Moses standing on top of Mount Sinai with the Ten Commandments, of Ruth caring for Naomi, and of Jesus calming the sea for the fishermen.

My evening ritual started with the reading of a few passages from the gospels. This was usually followed by either candle-gazing to improve my concentration or by a visualization to eliminate negative thoughtforms. Although thoughts of home and my former work sometimes intruded, these evenings were largely devoted to enhancing my spirituality.

altar with candles

I had just finished my Bible reading and had lit the candles when I noticed a being watching me from the corner of the room. It was not my leprechaun friend, nor was he one of the other elementals I had met. In fact, I was not sure he was an elemental at all. I was certain, however, that he was not human.

I felt myself begin to panic. I had fears of things that went bump in the night and evil entities with which I might have to do battle that summer. I steeled myself for a confrontation and, studying him closely, waited for him to make his intentions clear.

He was dressed in a very old-fashioned, simple black suit. He was not particularly tall, on the slender side, and was sitting cross-legged in a relaxed position. His white hands were folded across his lap. His head, however, was peculiar—bigger than average, round and hairless, with very small, seemingly-blind eyes. Yet I had no doubt that he saw me perfectly well.

He made no threatening gestures and my heart began to calm down. Perhaps sensing this, he began, "I mean you no harm. I have come to teach you many things that you do not know. We need to get started, so get up and get dressed—we're going out."

"Wait a minute," I said. It was eleven-thirty and I was tired. "Couldn't we do this tomorrow? And who are you, anyway?"

"Names are not important," he replied, striking a familiar chord. "As for waiting until tomorrow, I'm afraid that is not possible. Our work must take place at night."

Not yet persuaded to leave my warm bed to accompany this stranger into the cold, dark lane, I hesitated. "At least tell me where you're from, even if you don't want to tell me your name," I said firmly.

Unclasping his hands and stretching his long fingers towards me, he began, "You must suspend disbelief for the time being because you will have difficulty believing where I'm from." He was asking a lot. I preferred to maintain an active critical awareness to discern truth from untruth. I projected my thought towards him.

"Critical awareness is not the issue," he replied. "In order to learn, you will have to radically change your beliefs of what is and is not possible."

Not willing to be diverted from my original question, I asked again, "Who are you?"

Gazing at me with his blind eyes, he said calmly, "I'm a being from the center of the Earth." He paused for a moment to allow the impact of his words to sink in before continuing, "We are an old race on this planet—much older than humans—and we do not live in your dimension. We have little contact with humans but are aware of all changes that occur on this planet. We seek to work with humans who are helping to reestablish the natural balance of the Earth in accordance with spiritual laws. This you are doing, and that is the reason I'm here."

Although his visit was unexpected, I was not totally ignorant of his race.

"Many years ago, a friend lent me a book about your people," I said. "It was called *Etidorpha,* by John Uri Lloyd, and I was deeply moved by the book, as what I read sounded true. Although you're right, its concepts were so far removed from my reality that it created a lot of inner conflict for me. Then a strange thing happened. I gave back my borrowed copy and went to the bookstore to buy a new one. They said that they had never heard of it, nor could they find a record of the book in any catalogue."

He smiled wisely towards me and stated, "The being in that book who taught John Uri Lloyd was me. I am the ambassador to humans."

"How can that be?" I said. "That book was written over a hundred years ago."

"Like elementals, we have long lives," he answered. "Humans would have a much longer life span if they were attuned to the natural laws, as we and the elemental race are.

"So are you prepared to come with me?" he asked, and I knew that I had only seconds to make up my mind. I was very frightened by his request. Not only was I nervous about him, I was also worried about the elementals living in the lane who disliked humans. Since childhood I'd been frightened of beings coming for me in the dark. My natural hypersensitivity seemed even more acute at night, when I was more aware of beings from other realities. To prevent myself from slipping into them or letting them slip into my dimension, I had learned to shield myself. Walking outside at midnight with this strange being represented one of my worst fears. Still I knew that overcoming my fears was an essential part of my purpose for the summer. I must do it to become a conscious creator. I steeled myself and, with a leap of faith, hopped out of bed and reached for my clothes. He disappeared while I dressed and then, putting on my raincoat and scarf, I walked out into the cold night air. It was midnight.

Reappearing at my side, the humanoid being walked with me towards the lane. He turned left down the lane and I followed. Becoming accustomed to the dark, I looked at the sky and noticed that I was unable to recognize any of the beautiful stars. It was the first night that I'd seen them.

"Could you tell me a bit more about yourself?" I asked, desperate for information with which to anchor myself.

"Our race has mastered the elements in a way far superior to humans," he replied. "We can control the electromagnetic forces of the Earth to move in space and time and between dimensions."

"How does your control differ from that of the elementals?" I asked, wondering how many versions of traveling through space and time I was expected to learn in one summer

"We differ from elementals," he replied, "in that my race, like humans, are creators in training. Elementals as a race, as you have been told, are only now learning to become creators, but humans and my race have been on this path for millions of years. My race works with the hierarchy that oversees the evolution of all beings on this planet. This hierarchy is composed of members of the human, elemental, my race, and others. These members of the hierarchy have evolved within their own specific evolutions to become strong enough creators to determine the destiny of a planet like Earth. The specific role of my race, the beings inside the Earth, is to help the Earth develop as a sentient being."

"And where do humans fit into this plan?" I asked, worried that I might have to defend the actions of humanity again.

"When humans originally came to this planet, our race taught them to work with the earth element to create form. As the Earth became more solid, we started to withdraw inside to continue our evolution. Later, in Atlantis, a few of us still taught the laws of polarity and of working with the electromagnetic currents of the Earth. Unfortunately, this knowledge was used by misguided humans for their own purposes and Atlantis, as you know, was destroyed. We witnessed its destruction, as we see all that happens on the surface, and even warned those Atlantians who were working with the divine plan so they were able to escape to other places on the Earth. That, however, was the last time we assisted your entire race."

Absorbed in his story, I was surprised to notice that we had already come to the end of the lane. The choice was uphill to the cemetery, or down to the sea. I hoped he'd choose down. He chose up.

"So, if I understand correctly, the purpose of your race is to help the Earth itself to become sentient," I said. "But how does your purpose tie in with the purpose of humans?"

"Humans are learning to become creators, and they need raw material with which to work." He paused to think of an image with which I could identify. "Humans are like children playing in a sandbox and learning to build castles. The Earth provides the raw material."

"So," I said, "does your race travel from solar system to solar system, helping planets to become sentient?"

"Yes," he said, pleased. "That's exactly what we are learning to do. That is the path of our evolution as a race. Working with other beings who are evolving on the planet's surface is secondary. We do this only when specifically requested by the hierarchy."

"And this hierarchy," I asked, intrigued, "is the one composed of masters from human and elemental evolutions who oversee the evolution of all beings on Earth?"

"The very same," he replied. "We are members as well."

"Now," he said, changing the topic, "we need to begin your instruction. The first thing you must learn is that what you consider to be solid is not so. The reason I've come at night is because the veil between your reality and other realities is much thinner. You can do things that you would not believe possible during the day."

Stopping, he pointed to a hedge beside the road and said, "That hedge is not solid. You can walk right through it, and I'd like you to do so."

Holy hints of Castaneda, I thought, wondering if I'd be able to master the trick that Don Juan seemed intent on teaching Carlos. Thinking 'not solid, not solid,' I moved forward and crashed into the hedge. Stepping back, I searched for another technique. Letting my eyelids droop and my eyesight lose focus, I used my will combined with my powers of visualization to create a tunnel through the hedge.

I was about to try walking through this tunnel when I heard, "Stop! I don't want you to create a tunnel. That's what magicians do. If you do this you blast a hole in other dimensions that kills the life where that hole exists. Instead, you must see the reality of the hedge. It is composed mostly of vacant space and only a few atoms of material." As he spoke, he reached over and ran his arm easily through the hedge and back out again.

I tried to imagine doing what he had just done. I knew that what he did was possible. My problem was that I didn't believe that I could do it. I'd hit a wall. I thought back to my childhood when I had tried to fly like Peter Pan and failed. Even this summer, I had dutifully tried to light a fire in the hearth, using my mind. The result—failure. Halfheartedly I threw myself against the hedge and, as expected, failed again. Pulling my body off the thorns and brushing off my raincoat, I looked searchingly at my companion.

Arms akimbo, he stared at me in disgust and said, "That was a pathetic attempt."

"Maybe I'm afraid of losing control," I said. "I know that I can do it in other realities," I argued in my defense. "I just can't believe that it's possible in this one." Mentally, I compared myself to other humans I knew and was satisfied they could do no better. Besides, I was denser than my companion so it was no wonder that what worked for him did not work for me.

Extending his arm in front of me, he said, "Touch me."

I reached out, touched him, and to my surprise discovered that he was as solid as me.

"Now," he said, "touch me again."

I did so and my hand passed right through his arm. Turning to him, I awaited an explanation.

"It's simple," he stated, gazing at me with his blind, all-seeing eyes. "I can move my atoms into any configuration I choose. If I want to be more solid, I move them to my exterior. To be more porous, I disseminate them throughout my body. It's this principle that allows me to pass through the hedge, and you can do the same. Close your eyes and visualize your body becoming lighter, more porous. See the hedge doing the same. Now imagine yourself moving through the hedge so that your atoms do not collide."

I followed his instructions and visualized the image in my mind.

"Now, move through the hedge," he commanded.

Trying to hold the image, I moved forward and once again encountered the hedge.

"I don't seem to be able to do it," I said, exasperated.

"You did a lot better this time. Most humans are only conscious in the first three dimensions. You can see these as a stationary point, a line, and a cube. But there are twelve dimensions in all. Your etheric body, or body elemental, works in the fourth dimension and it has accomplished what you asked it to do. However, there is great resistance in your mind to believe that you can accomplish this in your third-dimensional reality. Even as you visualize yourself doing it, part of your mind is saying it can't do it."

He was absolutely correct. I was only too well aware of this internal dialogue but could think of no way to cancel my disbelief.

"Do I believe I can do it in higher dimensions?" I asked.

"Yes, of course," he replied. "Not in the emotional realm but in your higher mental and spiritual realms, it is already recorded that you've done it. It's just that most humans are not conscious above the fifth dimension. When I say 'above,' it's not entirely accurate because all dimensions exist simultaneously. It would be more accurate to say that the higher the dimension, the more pure and subtle the energies. You have access to these subtle vibrations much more than most and have employed your talents in listening to the higher dimensions to gain information for your book, *Decoding Destiny*. However, when you are personally involved, as you are in this experiment with the hedge, you are unable to set aside your beliefs in your third-dimensional reality to move into the higher realms.

I was disappointed in myself but didn't know how to transfer my belief to higher dimensions to overcome my experience of the "solid" physical world.

"We'll leave it at that for now, shall we?" he suggested.

Relieved, I agreed, and we continued our walk towards the cemetery. I was tired, wanting only to return to my warm bed.

We were almost at the cemetery when he stopped. "I think we've done enough for tonight," he said. "We can continue tomorrow, if you will come out again."

I nodded heartily and we turned and in silence started the long walk back to the cottage. I entered a time of no time where an hour feels like a minute. At the entrance to my gate, he paused. "I'll come for you at midnight tomorrow," he said, and disappeared.

In a daze, I walked up the path and into the cottage. Turning on the light, I saw that it was three-thirty. Hurriedly, I stripped off my clothes and collapsed onto the bed. The hot water bottles were still lukewarm. Hugging them to me, I fell into a deep, sound sleep.

CHAPTER TWENTY-ONE

The Ambassador Returns

 JERKED MYSELF AWAKE. I had been dreaming of wandering outside in the night with a being from the center of the Earth. Hold on, I thought, it had actually happened. I looked down at my scratched hands and remembered the hedge. Then, remembering my promise to meet the being again at midnight, I pulled the covers over my head and tried to go back to sleep.

Immediately I heard the leprechaun's voice, "No you don't," he said, frustrated. "I want to hear all about your visitor."

"When am I going to get some peace?" I groaned. "I've got you by day and now I've got him by night. Is it any wonder I'm not enlightened?"

Thinking of the humor in the situation, I started to chuckle and was quickly joined by my leprechaun friend. Still laughing, I pulled myself out of bed and headed for the toilet while mentally asking the leprechaun to wait for my return. I wondered, is this what everyone needs to go through in order to become enlightened? If so, I empathized with all the poor unsuspecting humans waiting innocently for their enlightenment experience.

Finished, I returned to the bedroom, grabbed a blanket off the bed, and threw it on the couch. I sat huddled under its heavy woolen warmth, and my leprechaun friend soon reappeared under the blanket with me.

"So," he exclaimed excitedly, "tell me all about it."

"How do you know that there's anything to tell?" I teased. "Maybe I had a quiet evening reading the Bible before retiring early."

"And I could be thinkin' of becoming a Christian," he responded quickly, giving it back.

"Seriously," I said, still smiling, "how do you know that I had a guest last night?"

He hesitated, blushing, and said, "I overheard a conversation."

"Between. . . ?" I prompted.

"Between the ambassador and one of my teachers," the eavesdropper replied, having trouble looking me in the eye.

Curiosity aroused, I inquired, "Is the ambassador to humans the same as the one to elementals?"

"No, we've got our own," he said.

"Why would the ambassador to elementals be speaking to an elemental master about the ambassador to humans visiting a human, unless," I paused for suspense, "they wanted you to overhear?" I was delighted at their joke and how easily he had fallen into the trap.

Casting aside the blanket and sitting up straight, he turned red in the face. "Why would they want to do that?" he demanded.

"So," I answered, hoping that my deduction was correct, "that you'd tell me all about the beings in the center of the Earth."

"Ummmm," he said, stroking his chin and smiling good-naturedly at the trick that had been played on him. "Could be you're right, so why don't I do that and help them along."

Pausing to gather his thoughts, he commenced. "There are ambassadors from the center of the Earth assigned to every race evolving on the planet. The ambassador to the elementals has been working with us from before my time. Unlike humans, elementals have known about the beings in the center of the Earth all along. They don't communicate with elementals generally, but talk to our masters and also to elementals who work directly with the earth element such as gnomes and dwarfs. Since our caste was formed, the ambassador has spoken to us many times."

"What is he teaching you?" I asked, eager to hear of the differences between my instruction and his.

"He's teaching us how to maintain the Earth's gravity and polarity. After his race leaves the Earth, elementals must be trained to do this job. He even took us to the center of the Earth to see what his people were doing. The ambassador is also teaching us to move atoms in our bodies so that we can become denser or lighter. I find that difficult." The leprechaun shrugged his shoulders in frustration.

"But I saw you put your hand through my mantelpiece, not to mention that you walk through my walls. Don't you move your atoms to do that?" I said to him in disbelief.

"No," my friend replied. "That's easy for me because elementals live in the fourth dimension. It's our equivalent of your third dimension. Now if I wanted to be seen by humans and be solid, like they think they're solid, in the third dimension, I can't do it. If I could move my atoms around like the ambassador said, I could appear solid like you."

Sympathizing, I was glad nevertheless that I wasn't the only one struggling with that exercise.

Turning to me, he asked, "And what did you learn last night?"

"He tried to teach me the same exercise that your ambassador is teaching you. I was not successful," I answered wistfully. "It must be important for both of our races to learn."

"If we can control the movement of our atoms, then we can travel to many more dimensions without affecting the life there," my leprechaun friend responded enthusiastically. "Your atoms and mine are mixing up every time we meet, and that changes both of us. When we talk and when we think about each other, our atoms move together. Neither of us can control this presently, and we must learn to if we're to travel to other dimensions and not intersect with the atoms of beings there. "

"How many dimensions and worlds do you travel to now?" I asked, intrigued.

"I'm conscious in three," he replied. "The elemental, human, and mineral worlds. I'm also learning to be conscious in the world of the being from the center of the Earth."

Listening to him, I thought of the worlds in which I was conscious and said, "I think I'm conscious in the human, angelic, and elemental worlds, and I'm learning to be conscious in the world of the masters."

"You've left out the world of the body elemental. You are conscious there as well," he reminded me.

"I've heard that there are twelve dimensions. Does that tally with your information?" I asked, eager to cross-check my sources.

"That's what I've been told as well," the leprechaun replied. "This being from the center of the Earth might teach you to control gravity and polarity. Did you know that they can grow any kind of crystals they wish?"

Suddenly I was overwhelmed by the amount of things that I was required to learn and pleaded, "Could we take the day off? I think I'd like to be rested when he comes back tonight."

"Of course," he replied, jumping to his feet. "I'll see you tomorrow." With these words he disappeared, leaving me alone to rest for the remainder of the day.

Staying awake until midnight was agony. I retired to bed late and with all my clothes on sat reading the Bible. Every half-hour I yawned and looked at my watch. I must have dozed off sitting up, because I woke just after midnight to find him sitting in the chair that he had occupied the previous night. Watching me, he waited patiently for me to fully wake up.

"Sorry," I said, groggily forcing myself into consciousness and adding by way of explanation, "I've never been a night owl."

"On the contrary, you are incredibly active at night. It's just that you don't remember it," he corrected me gently.

"I remember a lot of my dreams, if that's what you mean," I replied.

"You just remember what your body lying in the bed is doing," the being elaborated. "You do not remember where your consciousness goes or what it does."

"I'm confused," I said. "Is it my body elemental that stays in bed and looks after my body, and my higher consciousness that leaves?"

"That's exactly what happens," said the ambassador. "Your body elemental uses that time to integrate your memories for the day and often plays back images for you to digest and think about before they get stored. Meantime, your higher consciousness travels to other realms. We've met before during your nighttime travels, but you don't remember."

"My apologies. It slipped my mind." I smiled at him charmingly.

"Quite all right," he replied, bowing his head in acknowledgment before continuing. "One of the reasons that you sleep so many hours at night is that you have such a vibrant night consciousness. It's frustrated by the small amount of itself that it gets to employ in your daytime self—your personality, as you humans call it."

"Am I doing something wrong?" I asked, eager to amend my nonproductive habits.

"Partially, in that you sit on your talents too much," he replied, looking at me with his blank eyes. "But that's only part of the reason. The rest is that you work with all the kingdoms during the night and try to bring parts of each to the other. You are a messenger between the worlds. You aren't just learning, you're also teaching."

"No wonder I sometimes wake up exhausted," I said, in mock seriousness. "So have I been to visit you and your race at the center of the Earth?" I asked, already anticipating his answer.

"Many times," he replied. "That's one of the reasons you have such a deep love for and interest in crystals. We have taught you the talents of each one and how to program them to work with humans. That's why you could easily access that information for your book."

"If we have been working so well together in my sleeping consciousness, why have you decided to bring yourself into my waking consciousness?" I asked, puzzled.

"You've reached the stage in your evolution," he began, "when you can no longer split yourself to work with different worlds and dimensions. That is why I, your leprechaun friend, and your body elemental are here. Your day and night selves are merging."

"It seems to me that everyone knows more about me than I do about myself," I said, a little miffed.

"That's because of the split," he replied. "Elementals don't sleep and neither does our race. We don't have the same split as humans."

"Fascinating," I responded, surprised. "But why are humans split?"

"Humans call it the fall from grace—because you started using free will to choose destinies for yourselves," the ambassador continued. "By day, you strengthen your personalities, and by night, you work with your divine self. The stronger your personalities, the more you can give to your divine self. This is how humans evolve into being creators."

"You are creators as well," I said, reminding him of what he had told me the previous night. "How is your evolution different from that of humans?"

"My race learned to work with polarities and gravity when the Earth had barely manifested. It was a lot less solid and more gaseous than today. Through this work, we developed our talent and knowledge, and through our contact with other races, we developed flexibility of thought and wisdom. We've become creators, not by falling away from the divine plan, but by bringing more of its essence into manifestation. Your race is developing a different consciousness entirely."

I was taking in his words when he stood up and said, "I'm going to leave. Sleep on these thoughts tonight so that this information can bring together your two parts."

Just as I sighed with relief at the prospect of an easy night, he continued, "I'll not be back tomorrow, but I have an assignment for you. I want you to go out at midnight to the cemetery—the old Irish one. Then walk farther along the road to the ancient dolmen and spend the night there. This exercise will help you remove your fear of things that go bump in the night."

With these words, he bowed his head slightly and left the bedroom. I heard no door open or close, but knew he was gone.

A reprieve from hell, I thought, already anxious about the following night's ordeal. I was terrified of the cemetery and even more terrified of spending the night at the four gigantic standing stones that made up the ancient dolmen, which was likely a place for secret initiations in the ancient world. Taking off my clothes and sliding back into bed, my last thought was that I would probably be too scared to sleep.

CHAPTER TWENTY-TWO

Vision Quest

LL NEXT DAY, I STEWED. I tried to meditate, but couldn't. I went to the village to buy groceries, and that took my mind off things for about an hour. Needless to say, my leprechaun friend was noticeably absent.

All day I felt the energy build around me. I had no doubt that this night was to be profoundly important. But there was nothing that terrified me more than spending a night by myself in the cemetery. Often, I felt that I was leading a Jekyll and Hyde existence. To Mrs. O'Toole and the villagers, I was a tourist renting the Davidson cottage and that, certainly, was part of my reality. What, however, would they say if they knew I spent my nights wandering the lanes and visiting graveyards. Obviously there was no one I could speak to about my fear. I was on my own.

I ate little dinner and as midnight approached I debated not going at all. It was raining, cold, and dark outside, and my bed was warm and safe. I even tried convincing myself that I had imagined the ambassador's visits. But if I doubted his existence, then I'd have to doubt the reality of my entire summer with the leprechaun—as well as all experiences I'd had since childhood. No, there was too much evidence attesting to the reality of these other worlds.

Also, I knew—absolutely knew—that this nighttime vision quest was connected to my desire for enlightenment. There really was no choice; I had to face my fears.

155

Just before midnight I dressed as warmly as I could, wearing my water-resistant raincoat and scarf. Opening the door, I set out alone. The rain had not abated and, with no moon or stars lighting the sky, it was almost pitch black. Within minutes my glasses were so wet that I could barely see where I was going. Virtually blind, I shuffled along the lane, trying not to fall into the ditches, which were high with water. My shoes sank into puddle after puddle along the pot-holed lane, and my feet were soaked.

I tried to ignore my bodily discomfort and my consciousness swept the lane for any goblins who might be lying in wait for me. I felt their presence and steeled myself for an attack. If, in my vulnerable state, they wanted to confront me, this would be the perfect time. Enduring the rain, I forged ahead, treading the paths I had walked so often by day. Each cold soggy step brought me closer to the cemetery, and finally I arrived at my destination. The gate loomed ahead and, visualizing a psychic shield of protection around me, I unlatched it and entered.

Immediately I was confronted by a myriad of ghosts—the unhappy dead. For the first time since I'd left the cottage, I heard an inner voice.

"Sit down on the gravestone in the middle," it said.

I did not recognize the voice as belonging to one of the beings with whom I was working. Still, I knew it was to be obeyed and, following the instruction, searched for the correct stone and sat down. The spirits continued to follow me. Some were weeping, and some held knives, which they threatened to use on me. I was scared out of my wits and, holding my breath, reinforced my protective shield.

"Lower your shield," the voice said. "You must love these spirits and help them as you did your thoughtforms. They are stuck. They believe they're either in hell or still alive. You must convince them that they are dead and help them to see the angels who are waiting to take them to their next home."

I could imagine lowering my shield to the sobbing women and

lost ones. It was quite another matter to face the men who were trying to stab me.

"It's essential that you do this or you will always be afraid," I heard the voice say.

I will stay shielded with love, I decided, bringing my shield into my heart, where it felt secure. I knew that I could use my etheric body to defend myself, if necessary.

"Stop!" I called out to the spirits hovering around me. "You must listen."

They stopped to look at me, but I could tell that they were scattered and unfocused. One of the menacing male spirits raised his hand to strike me with his knife. Grabbing his wrist I said, "Stop. I am here to help you."

He paused, and I could tell that my will helped hold him in place. Some of the others were unconvinced and lunged at me. Many arms came out of my body and held the etheric wrists and arms of my assailants. Now I had everyone's attention.

"You are all dead," I said, getting right to the point, as I had no idea how long they could focus.

At once, the women started wailing and ripping their ghostly garments. The men struggled harder to kill me. I opened my heart, flooding them with love, and they immediately calmed down.

"I don't believe you," the ringleader spat at me.

"Look around you," I invited all of them. "You are in a cemetery and, if you look, some of you will find your names on the stones."

There was a scurry of activity as the spirits dispersed around the cemetery to look for their markers.

"Here's mine," I heard, over to the right.

"I've found mine," sobbed a woman to my left.

Not all the spirits were convinced. I mentally sent out a call for help from the angels who help departed souls. They arrived instantly and stood on the outskirts of the cemetery.

"Do you see the angels?" I asked the spirits. Most nodded and

I continued, "They will take care of you. Go with them and they will help you rejoin your loved ones."

Most moved forward and, immediately embraced by angels, disappeared. However, a few recalcitrant spirits hung back and refused to go.

"You can do no more here," I heard the voice say. "Come."

I stood up and headed for the gate. Turning back, I saw the few remaining spirits watching me. They still held on to their anger and rage and were unable to depart the Earth. Closing the gate, I turned left and continued along the lane that led to the dolmen.

Soggy and barely able to see, I trudged along. I was proud of myself for facing the spirits of the cemetery, and also felt grateful that I had been able to help them. So often, I thought, we get caught up in our own fears and lose track of what we can do to help others. I was still thinking of this when I arrived at a fork in the lane. Up a steep path to my left was the dolmen.

Turning left, I started up the path and immediately slipped and fell. Down on my hands and knees and now totally soaked,

dolmen for initiation

I realized that what had once been a path had in the rain turned into a small stream. Pulling myself to my feet, I was starting to move forward again when I heard, "Lie face down and humble yourself."

It was the same voice I'd heard in the cemetery and it brooked no argument. I lay face down in the muddy stream and let the water course down my neck and chest. An image of Jesus, carrying his cross to Golgatha, leapt into my mind. Some parallel experience was occurring to me this night. I'd asked for a journey of initiation and I'd got it. Perversely, this thought lifted my spirits. Getting to my feet, I wiped off my glasses on the grass and continued uphill. Through walking, stumbling, and some crawling on my hands and knees, I finally reached the dolmen.

Like most of its sisters in this part of the country, the dolmen was probably at least five thousand years old. It was composed of four standing stones, three of which lay on their sides to form three walls of a building. The fourth and largest stone lay flat and formed a roof above the other three. The structure resembled a little cave—or a coffin.

The dolmen was surrounded by a barbed-wire fence. Originally, it was probably intended to keep out the sheep, but it was no longer intact.

"Pierce your finger on the fence and draw blood," I heard the voice say.

My hands were filthy and the barbed-wire fence was rusty. What serious infection was I exposing myself to, I wondered. Still, a blood offering was appropriate. They must have had similar rituals in former times when the dolmens were used for initiation. Also, I reminded myself, Jesus had his head pierced with a crown of thorns. With my index finger, I pushed down on one of the barbs. Nothing happened. The barbs were dulled with rust, and I needed to push harder. Feeling slightly sick, I tried again and, to make sure of success, ripped my finger along the wire. I achieved only a deep scratch, not an open wound, and hoped that this was enough.

"Touch all your chakra points with this finger," I heard.

I hastened to do this and starting at the base of my spine touched my root chakra, moved to my sexual chakra, my solar plexus, heart centre, throat centre, third eye, and finished with the crown chakra on top of my head. While doing this, I visualized opening each of these spiritual energy centres so that I could better serve all sentient beings on this planet. Finished, I sensed that I was to go to the dolmen. I didn't hear a voice this time but felt a strong tug in that direction.

Crouching down, I entered the dolmen coffin and sat between the stone walls. I could smell the sheep that had sheltered there out of the rain, and tried not to think about what I might be sitting on. Taking off my glasses, I proceeded to meditate. A guardian from another time appeared. He was dressed in rough woolen clothes and looked as filthy as me. He accepted my presence and I realized that he had taken many people on a journey of initiation in this very place. Raising a staff, he pointed behind me. The stone at my back opened to reveal a tunnel and he commanded me to enter.

I did as instructed and almost lost consciousness. In a dream-like state, people from both my present life and other lives drifted before me. Visions of what I had done in many lives floated by like snapshots. I knew that I wasn't to try to enter any of these lives but to simply observe them objectively. In seeing these lives, I was able to see the patterns, strengths, and weaknesses that echoed in my present life. I saw who I was in a detached way. It was as if I were judging myself more completely than anyone else could judge me. Simultaneously I realized that this is what happens during the third initiation, when the beings who help us with our evolution decide if we are ready to become co-workers with them. These experiences have always been a secret part of the mysteries that all humans undergo on the journey to become creators. How long I was there, I couldn't say. Finally, I became aware of my cold wet body and returned to waking consciousness, huddled in the dolmen.

"Leave your glasses and come back in the morning," said the voice.

Stooping, I emerged from the dolmen and tried to make out the path home. Everything was a blur. It was still raining heavily and was pitch black. I could see nothing without my glasses. I hesitated momentarily about leaving them but decided to continue following the instructions. It was symbolic that I was asked to trust that I could see without my glasses. I was asked to use a different kind of sight. Sliding and slipping, I made my way to the lane. With the rain streaming down my face, I trudged in a trancelike state back to my cottage. The light was just venturing over the eastern hills when I reached my gate, and I was thankful to be home before my neighbors woke. Peeling off my wet clothes with numb fingers, I filled up the water bottles and climbed into bed. I lay there for a few moments in a semi-numb state, utterly exhausted, yet filled to the brim with feelings of accomplishment. I had done what was asked of me.

CHAPTER TWENTY-THREE

The Bikers Arrive

 KNOCK ON THE DOOR jerked me back from a deep sleep. Struggling to consciousness, I looked at my watch and discovered it was ten-thirty. A second knock. Grabbing the blanket from the bed, I wrapped it around me and shuffled to the door. A tall young man, dressed from head to toe in black leather and carrying a motorcycle helmet under his arm, stood at the entrance.

"Hello, I'm the owner's son, Robert Davidson," he said, smiling. "My mates and I have come up from Dublin for a few days and wondered if we could camp out at the back." As he spoke, two other young men, similarly dressed, walked into view.

"You're welcome to camp," I replied, "but don't you think it's a bit wet?" It was still drizzling from the previous night.

"Naw, we don't mind," he said. He was about twenty-one, still at the age where being tough mattered.

Just as he was turning his back to leave, my mouth flew open and spoke, "Would you and your mates like to come for dinner?"

"Love to," Robert replied, and the other two nodded their heads.

"One o'clock?" I suggested. Dinner in old rural Ireland was at midday, with something lighter eaten in the evening.

"Right," he replied, and strode off to wheel the motorcycles into the yard.

It was a treat to have company, but I wondered how I'd be able to pull it off in time. Not only that, but I'd forgotten all about

162

leaving my glasses at the dolmen. Now I wouldn't be able to get them until later in the afternoon. I prayed silently that they were still there. Without them, I could only see clearly for about three feet in front of me. I could have put in my contacts, but I resisted, knowing I must practice seeing differently.

Dragging the blanket back into the bedroom, I discovered my wet clothes from the previous night lying in a heap on the floor. I turned them over with my foot. They were filthy. I went to the dresser and pulled out some dry jeans and a top. Somehow I would have to get through the next couple of days without the Aran sweater. Gingerly picking up the sodden sweater, jeans, and rain-coat, I dumped them in the tub and washed them out as best I could. I hung the blue jeans over the towel bar and laid the sweater flat on a towel. I then carried my raincoat into the living room, where it could dry out once the fire had been lit.

Returning to the kitchen, I searched the fridge for food. There was a hunk of lamb, and some potatoes, carrots, and onions. Lamb stew it would be. That and some soda bread would do the trick. I'd just put the stew on to cook when I caught sight of Mrs. O'Toole coming in the gate. Her timing, as always, was perfect.

"Mrs. O'Toole," I greeted her warmly, opening the door. "I'm so glad to see you. Robert Davidson is here with two of his mates. Can you come for dinner?"

"Paddy said that he saw them comin' down the lane this mornin'," she replied, not answering my question. "So I came over to see how they were doin'."

"They're camping," I answered, smiling as she rolled her eyes heavenward.

"So, will you come for dinner at one?" I completed my invitation. I had known Mrs. O'Toole for almost a month, and I'd only ever offered her chocolate, biscuits, and tea.

"That'd be nice," she smiled, delighted. "I might as well put on the fire while I'm here, then."

Company, a warm fire—it felt like a celebration for what I had accomplished the previous night. However, I had no intention of sharing the details of my incredible experience with my dinner guests. As Mrs. O'Toole got the fire going, I straightened up the living room, put away the book on faeries, and started to set the table.

Mrs. O'Toole caught my eye as she was going out the door and said, "I'll be back at one."

I wonder why she doesn't just stay, I thought to myself. The answer came quickly enough. Promptly at one, Mrs. O'Toole arrived, wearing her Sunday best. Taking off a new raincoat and her wellies at the door, she put on her church shoes. The boys and I were still dressed in our casual clothes—they in black leather, and me in jeans. My Aran sweater, raincoat, and shoes steamed in front of the fire, adding to the cozy, homey atmosphere. "Mrs. O'Toole, it's good to see you again," said Robert, getting up from his chair and extending his hand in greeting. He then proceeded to introduce her to his friends. She smiled happily as if she were the belle of the ball. It was wonderful to see her being fussed over. She didn't have an easy life, and to go out for dinner was something special. I'd become very fond of Mrs. O'Toole and was not looking forward to leaving the cottage.

Pushing that thought out of my mind, I asked Robert, "How long have you known Mrs. O'Toole?"

"Ever since we got the cottage, which was," he paused, turning to Mrs. O'Toole, "twenty years ago, wasn't it?"

"Aye, you were just a wee thing then," Mrs. O'Toole replied, giving him a mischievous little dig.

He blushed a bit, but grinned good-humoredly. Leaving them to entertain themselves, I went to get the stew.

Robert's two friends didn't say much but, judging from their appetites, they enjoyed their meal. I didn't expect them to have much in common with an Irish country woman and a Canadian tourist. However, the conversation was kept going by Robert and Mrs. O'Toole reminiscing about the changes to the village over the last twenty years.

"Do you remember the winter we had that terrible storm and our roof caved in?" Robert asked Mrs. O'Toole.

"That was the worst winter we've had in these parts," she replied. "What a mess it was gettin' it fixed with it rainin' all the time."

The weather hadn't changed, I thought to myself. It was thoroughly enjoyable listening to their history. I'd never seen Mrs. O'Toole so chatty. Throughout dinner they'd been weaving through stories of the past and had now progressed to the present.

"We've a craft shop now in town. Paddy's sister Mary opened it," Mrs. O'Toole said.

I'd been there. It was in a shack near the Unicorn and consisted mostly of hand-knit babies' booties and kitchen ceramics. I didn't think it would bolster the tourist trade but decided not to comment.

"We'll have to visit it then, won't we lads," replied Robert. With that, he got up from the table and, thanking me for the meal, strolled out the door, followed by his friends. Mrs. O'Toole walked over to her wellies and put them on. Taking her scarf from her pocket, she donned her best raincoat and said, "Thank ya for the meal. 'Twas good," then turned and left.

Over my shoulder I heard, "I always liked Robert. What did you think of him?"

My leprechaun friend was seated in his usual place, with his feet up on the couch and hands clasped behind his head. I walked over to join him and was just on the point of sitting down when he jumped up and said, "No, no, no. No time for that; you've got to get your glasses."

As usual, he seemed fully informed of my life. Not for the first time I wondered what he did when he was not with me. I was just starting to ask that very question when he repeated, "Your glasses."

Looking outside at the steady downpour, I replied, "Maybe it will clear a bit later."

"No chance of that. Come on, put on your raincoat and shoes and get going."

"The raincoat and shoes are still wet from last night," I replied and pointed to them steaming by the fire.

"Then they won't get any wetter, will they?" said the leprechaun impassively.

"You're right there," I said, sticking my foot into a soggy shoe. "I don't suppose you'd like to keep me company."

Hesitating, he walked over to the window and looked out at the rain. "I usually don't go out in 'inclement' weather," he said, and I could tell by his emphasis that he was trying out a new word.

"However, for you . . ." he added, leaving the sentence hanging.

"I'm forever grateful, sir," I said, bending over to put on my other shoe. Reaching for my wet raincoat, I noticed that the leprechaun had already dressed in sturdy raingear. A big pair of wellies came up past his knees, a fisherman's black oilskin raincoat covered the rest of him, and his top hat had been replaced by a large, broad-brimmed sou'wester.

"I wish you'd get me an outfit like yours," I sighed, sloshing towards the door.

"Just one of the little perks of being an elemental," he chuckled, following me out into the rain.

"So, how did you enjoy your night of initiation? Are you enlightened yet?" the leprechaun chortled as we turned into the lane.

"Do I look different to you?" I asked, certain that he would notice if I did.

"Nope," he said, peering at me from under the brim of his hat.

"No, I don't think I became enlightened," I responded. "I think I'd feel differently if I had. There weren't any blinding flashes of light, just slogging through muddy water. However, strangely enough, I don't mind any more. I'm really quite proud of myself for sitting in the cemetery and dolmen all night and helping the spirits of the dead. Also, I feel like I've done what was expected of me."

"Dead people, yuck!" replied the leprechaun in disgust. "You wouldn't catch me anywhere near a haunted graveyard."

Smiling, I asked, "Don't you elementals have ghosts?"

"We do have elementals who lose their bodies by accident and you can hear them calling or reenacting the same thing over and over again," he answered. "But there aren't any rotting bodies in our world. That's repulsive. Our bodies all go back to the Void where they dematerialize so that their energy can be used again."

"I agree with you," I replied. "I'm all in favor of cremation. Get rid of the body so the person doesn't hang around trying to get back into it."

We were approaching the cemetery as we spoke. I was happy that I'd faced my fears there but hoped it would not be necessary to repeat the experience.

Reading my thoughts, the leprechaun said, "I think you're very brave. Do you think the masters will make me do the same on my dark night of initiation?"

"I can't say," I replied. "Humans need to face their worst fears before they can become enlightened. I imagine that there's a similar process for elementals. What is your worst fear?"

"That I'll fail—that I won't become a creator. That I've given up my life of joy and play for a life of duty and responsibility, and that it was useless 'cos I failed," the leprechaun answered.

I could tell from his serious tone that for him this would be a terrible blow. What did I have to worry about, I thought. Hundreds of thousands of humans must have become conscious creators by now, so at least I knew that I'd achieve it, given time. My leprechaun friend, being the first of his kind, had no such assurance. At that moment, I decided to redouble my energies to help him and his race.

During our talk, the rain continued to pour down. We were now approaching the dolmen—or, at least, where I vaguely remembered the dolmen to be. I would be so glad to find my glasses. Just as we started our ascent, I hazily made out two people coming towards me. They looked like a man and a woman.

"Are you going to the dolmen?" the man asked in a North American accent. Tourists, I thought. Strange how I no longer thought of myself as one of them.

"Yes," I replied, adding on impulse, "I think I might have left my glasses there."

"Oh, we found them," the woman said. "We put them on top of the stone so they wouldn't get broken."

"Thank you very much," I said, happy that they didn't inquire what they were doing there, and continued sloshing through the water up the hill to the dolmen. I found my glasses and, with a huge sigh of relief, put them on, only to discover that with the heavy rain, they improved my vision only slightly. I debated walking around without them for a few days to see what it did to my perception,

"A good idea," replied the leprechaun. "If you don't mind, I think I'll be going now. I'll see you tonight when Robert comes."

Robert had not said that he'd be coming, but I knew better than to question the leprechaun on his sources of information. Tired, I turned and headed back to the cottage. It seemed like a much longer walk without my friend. Thankfully, the fire was still burning when I arrived. I added more turf, lay down on the couch, and went to sleep.

CHAPTER TWENTY-FOUR

A Fireside Chat

T WAS ALMOST DARK WHEN I AWOKE. Looking at my watch, I saw that it was eight o'clock. I heaped more turf on the fire and cleaned off the dining-room table. I had just finished the dishes when there was a knock at the door. Opening it, I saw Robert standing in the rain, looking miserable.

"Do you mind if I come in and dry off in front of the fire?" he asked. "My mates have gone on to the pub and I'll be joining them later."

"Not at all—please come in," I said, stepping aside. Although it was still raining and depressing outside, I think he was looking for an excuse to relive his old life in the cottage. The fact that he had come now, less than a week before the arrival of the new owners, indicated that.

"Would you like some tea?" I asked.

"Yes, I'd love some," he replied, "and do you have any apples?"

"A couple, would you like them?"

"Have you ever had roasted apples?" he asked, and I knew he was recalling a childhood treat he had enjoyed in the cottage.

"No, I haven't, but I'd be glad to try one," I answered, bringing him the apples and watching while he skewered them on the fire poker and put them over the burning turf.

I saw his eyes roam the room, taking in every precious object. I brought in the tea and sat down. Wanting to give him an opportunity to talk, I asked, "Is there anything that you want to take away with you?"

"Naw, Mum and Dad will be up to get everything," he replied, trying to downplay his attachment.

At that very moment the leprechaun arrived and sat down beside me in his usual seat.

"Tell Robert that you've got the cottage for the rest of the summer," he urged.

I ignored him and asked Robert, "How do you like your tea?"

"With milk and sugar," he replied.

"Tell Robert that you've got the cottage for the summer," repeated the leprechaun, more loudly.

"How are the apples doing?" I asked Robert, while sending a mental message to my leprechaun friend, telling him to stop interrupting me.

"I think they're ready. Here's yours," said Robert, sliding a steaming, mushy apple into my saucer. The leprechaun sat beside me, his face reddening. He was not used to being thwarted.

"Excellent," I pronounced, taking a bite and extending my plate towards the leprechaun as a peace offering. Reaching down, he broke off a piece with his fingers and sat back savoring it.

"This is very important," he began again.

"I can't say that," I said mentally to the leprechaun. "He'll think I'm the most arrogant, selfish person he's ever met."

"Tell him that I told you to say it," retorted the leprechaun.

"Then he'll think I'm crazy," I thought at the leprechaun and aloud said to Robert, "That was the best apple I've ever tasted."

"Now!" commanded the leprechaun.

Irritated by his persistence, yet trusting that he must have had a good reason for this, I reluctantly said to Robert, "I'm glad you're sitting down because there's something I want to tell you that you might find a bit difficult to believe."

Robert looked at me quizzically while I struggled to find the right words.

"There's a leprechaun sitting beside me . . ." I began.

"Really? That's amazing. Does he live in the cottage?" interrupted Robert enthusiastically.

This was going to be easier than I'd thought. "Yes, he does, with his family," I replied.

"What does he think of my family?" asked Robert.

"Tell him that I've really enjoyed all of them and will be sorry to see them go," replied the leprechaun. "Oh, and just so he believes you, tell him that I really like his poetry."

I repeated all the leprechaun had said and Robert, laughing, admitted, "I haven't written much poetry lately."

He then proceeded to recite one of his poems about Achill Island. It was good, Yeats-like. There was definitely a touch of the mystic in Robert. Ireland had rooted itself in his blood and I could not see a career with an airline, like that of his father, in store for him. The leprechaun had relaxed and was enjoying our evening together, but he wasn't going to leave me in peace.

"Now tell him you've got the cottage for the rest of the summer," he pushed.

"Robert," I said, "the leprechaun wants me to tell you that I have the cottage for the rest of the summer."

He looked down at his feet and spoke sadly. "That's impossible. The cottage has been sold to a French couple who are living in a cottage owned by Heinrich Boll, the German author. Anyway, Heinrich Boll's coming back in a week and they've got to move out of his place and in here. You've only got another five days."

I certainly didn't want to leave and had, with all the other things I'd been dealing with that summer, put off thinking about it. Still, I knew I had no choice. The leprechaun was putting me in a very awkward position.

"I'll leave on time," I said to Robert, so he wouldn't be concerned. "However, if something happens that makes it possible for me to stay, please remember that I would like to."

"Of course," replied Robert, "but nothing will change."

"I've lived with the leprechaun too long to believe that," I said, defending my friend. "Time does not have the same meaning for him as it does for us. He can see what is going to happen in the future and how things will work out."

Robert stood to leave, "I must be going—time for the pub," he said and added, in the direction of the leprechaun, "Tell him I've enjoyed living here."

"He heard you and says for you to keep on writing poetry," I replied, showing Robert to the door.

Returning to the couch, I sat down beside my friend and asked, "What's going to happen?"

"Nice boy," he responded and winked. "See you tomorrow," he said and disappeared.

That little imp, I thought. He's just paying me back for refusing to ask Robert for the cottage. I wondered if Robert would tell his friends and family about the leprechaun and decided that he probably would. I was sure he'd meet with a variety of responses.

cottage entrance

Sitting down again and watching the smouldering turf, I pondered my options if the leprechaun was not right and I had to leave. No longer did I have the goal of enlightenment. If nothing else, I'd been cured of that desire. It had already been an unforgettable summer. I could always fly to Cyprus or Greece and lie in the sun. Bor-ring. It would be much more intriguing to remain right where I was and continue learning about elementals.

I retired to bed with nothing resolved. Eating breakfast the next morning, I still had not come up with a solution.

As I finished my toasted soda bread, I heard a tentative knock on the door and recognized it as Robert's. Opening the door, I smiled and said, "Good morning."

He was rather pale. Too much to drink last night, I thought. Without a word, he raised the morning paper in front of my face. The headline read, "Heinrich Boll dead." Robert was obviously shaken and waiting for an explanation.

"Neither I nor the leprechaun killed Heinrich Boll," I said, taken aback and attempting to lighten the situation. "As I told you last night, he can tell what's going to happen before it occurs."

Robert considered what I said and the color started to return to his cheeks.

"We're leaving for Dublin now," he said. "I'll tell Dad about you having the cottage for the next month."

"Thanks Robert," I replied, grateful for his intercession on my behalf.

Three days later, I received a letter from Mr. Davidson. My stay at the cottage had been extended for August.

Afterword

I N THE TEN YEARS SINCE THE SUMMER IN IRELAND, the leprechaun has visited me in Canada on a regular basis. Unlike humans, he is not confined to time and space and has called on me from Toronto to Nova Scotia and finally in Vancouver where I now reside. His favorite time to visit, not surprisingly, is mornings for tea and toast. Sometimes, wrapped up in daily work, I don't see him for days or weeks at a time, but when I call him with my mind, he almost always comes.

Nor are our visits confined to my home. He loves to accompany me on walks in the forest and much prefers trees and shade to open sunny beaches and, over time, my preferences have shifted to accompany his own. Since meeting him, I find I need more time alone and more time in natural settings. I try not to work in the summers, going instead to cottages where, rather than sleeping in a bed, I sleep under the stars and dream the important dreams.

Much has happened since my return from Ireland. At the end of that summer, I arrived in Canada so empty that I no longer had any goals at all—not even enlightenment. Shortly after my return, visiting with a Tibetan Buddhist friend, Zasep Tulku Rinpoche, I mentioned my lack of goals.

"That's wonderful," he replied, beaming.

Evidently this was seen as progress on the road to enlightenment, but at that moment I just felt empty. Rinpoche's comment, added to my lonely trials in Ireland, overwhelmed me and I started to cry. Between sobs I was able to respond, "But there's nothing I want to do anymore. I've even given up the goal of enlightenment."

Rinpoche looked at me with deep concern and I heard his thought. He wondered if I was giving up the desire to live, a kind of passive suicide.

This struck me as so amusing that I started to laugh and quickly reassured him by saying, "Don't worry, I'm not going to kill myself—but I don't know what to do either."

"Why don't you do something small that attracts you," he said and added, "Don't look for something big."

In my mind I saw all the countries and sacred sites of the world that I loved visiting and at that moment decided to invite people to go with me. The first country we visited was Ireland, of course. Since then I've been back to Ireland several times and my leprechaun friend has often accompanied me. Every year he informs me of his preference for the country I should visit next, and he has introduced me to elementals around the world.

I've come to realize over the last ten years that these tours are important, not just to the people who join me, but in helping to open up the energy centers of the Earth, both to heal the Earth and to bring ancient wisdom back into our world. This is for the good not only of humans but also of elementals. Over the years I've also noticed an increasing desire among people to learn about elementals. This seems to go hand-in-hand with our increased concern for the environment and our interest in other life forms.

Touring, counselling, and organizational consulting had kept me so busy during these ten years that I'd forgotten about my promise to write a book. My elemental friend did not forget, however, and in the summer of 1995, a decade after my stay in Ireland, he reminded me that it was now time.

Recalling my promise, I dutifully went into retreat to do so, full of assurances from my friend that it would be effortless. Writing about our first month together was remarkably easy and my friend came daily to take me back to our time in Ireland, enabling complete recall.

However, as soon as I had written the last chapter, A Fireside Chat, I could feel the book being closed and I could no longer write. The leprechaun absented himself for days, then weeks, and finally months, while I waited patiently to hear whether we were continuing with the story.

One day, while making blueberry pancakes back in my Vancouver home, I heard a voice chirp behind me, "Put on one for me and don't forget that maple syrup."

I turned and found my leprechaun friend seated at the table, awaiting his breakfast.

"So nice to see you again," I said, not without sarcasm.

"Don't scold. It's very unbecoming," he replied, frowning, and continued, "If you only knew what I've been through these last few days."

"You mean months, don't you?" I retorted, not ready to be mollified.

"Has it been that long here?" he inquired, looking out the window at the yellow and red leaves on the ground.

"Well, I guess it has," the leprechaun sighed and, looking at me, continued, "So I guess we'd best get back to what we were doing."

Knowing that no apology would be forthcoming—as he had yet to learn that human women desire such things—I let go of the expectation and awaited his news.

"I'm all ears," I smilingly replied, while visualizing the growth of long elfin ears.

"You're going to do that one too many times and be stuck with them," he chuckled, enjoying himself.

"I guess you're wondering if we're going to tell the story of the rest of the summer?" he said without preamble.

"Yes, and. . . ?" I asked, knowing that the answer was connected with his long absence.

"No," he answered and, before I could get a word in, waved his hand in the air, begging me to postpone judgment. "I've been trying to get agreement with the other elementals since I last saw you but they do not want to tell their part of the story now."

"But, why?" I inquired.

"There's a correct timing for all things and the time is right to share only what we've written. Ten years ago humans were not ready to even hear about elementals, and now they are. Since that time many books have been published on angels and now humans believe in them more than ever before. Likewise, humans are more willing to believe in beings from other planets than they were a decade ago and, because of this, they will be more willing to believe in elementals."

"All the more reason to say as much as we can right now, don't you think?"

"Not at all," answered the leprechaun, smiling at my attempt to change his mind. "All the more reason to say just the right amount so as not to lose our credibility. You must trust us and our timing in this matter."

"But you said a moment ago that you had been trying to convince the other elementals to proceed."

"Because of my work with you and my years studying humans, I have more hope for what we can accomplish now than do some of the other elementals," said the leprechaun. "They wish to wait for a better time for their part of the story to be received."

"I'm not happy with that decision," I replied. "Look, I trust you. I've had enough years with you to see that there are reasons—which I don't fully comprehend—for what you do. But," and I paused to emphasize my point, "humans are not like elementals. If we say that we're going to tell a story covering the whole summer, the readers want to hear about the second month."

The leprechaun weighed what I said and squinted his bushy brows together trying to understand my predicament.

"This book is called *Summer with the Leprechauns* not *Summer with the Elementals,* so we did do what we promised," said the leprechaun, trying to win me over to his side.

"True," I thought, but I was not entirely convinced. The leprechaun, noticing my response, put his head in his hands and, shaking it from side to side, exclaimed, "Humans! What is it about you humans that you lock yourself into doing what you promise even when the circumstances change and it becomes the wrong thing to do. And not only that," he wagged his finger at me, "humans always think they're missing out on something, and that having more is better.

"Besides, this will be practice for you to wean yourself away from doing everything you say you'll do. Treat this like an exercise."

Finishing his tirade, he sat back in his chair and, noticing my reaction to his lecture, softened his glance. Lucky he did, because I was just at the point of retorting about fickle, unreliable elementals that trick humans into doing what they want and don't deliver what they promise.

Reading my mind, my friend took a big breath and, acknowledging my point of view, said, "I see that we are placing you in a difficult position, but I believe that the readers will understand our reasons. We're at a crucial time in our evolutions together," he said, adding with a smirk, "We're just dating; we haven't as yet gotten married, so we still need to court each other to prove our good intentions."

"It seems to me that you've been a part of my life for longer than most people are married," I replied, softening slightly.

"And what if I refuse to stop writing," I added, throwing down the gauntlet.

"I wouldn't recommend that," he replied, the hint of a threat in his voice. "Remember what happened to you this summer when you overrode our directions."

How could I forget. The leprechaun had made life difficult for me not once, but three times. He had specifically told me not to read any of the book to others when I was writing. I had gone into retreat alone at a friend's cottage. During the day I wrote on my computer, and in the late afternoon another friend visited me, bringing food and relieving my isolation. Being a curious woman, this friend asked to read the manuscript and I, having a hard time disappointing people, said "yes." I turned on the printer to make a copy of the manuscript for her to read, only to discover that the printer wasn't working. I'd never had a problem with the printer before, and there seemed to be no reason for its malfunction. I refused to get the message and spent three days looking for people on the island to fix it, all without success. When I returned to Vancouver, my printer worked just fine.

Two weeks later, printer in tow, I took three ferries to get to another cottage to continue my writing in seclusion. The people who rented me the cottage had their twelve-year-old nephew visiting and I mentioned to him that I was writing a book about leprechauns. Not surprisingly, he wanted to read it and, not having learned my lesson the first time, again I said "yes." This time the printer ran out of toner on the third page and, unable to purchase any on the island, I was left for two weeks with a non-functioning printer.

The third and last time that I overrode the leprechaun's directions had its own special twist. I'd finished writing the book, as far as they'd let me, but I had decided to continue writing about the second month on my own. I went into retreat at a third cottage, this one even more remote than the other two. Thinking I'd outsmart the elementals, I did not take the printer to the third cottage. Instead, I printed the entire manuscript before leaving and took only my computer. Arriving at the cottage, I plugged in the computer and turned it on. Nothing. *Nada.*

For the rest of the week, I dutifully turned on the computer every day to see if the elementals had changed their mind. I had no doubt they were responsible for what was happening. The computer never worked, no matter where I plugged it in. After a week, I gave up and returned home. When I plugged in the computer, it worked perfectly.

The leprechaun had never before brought up these instances. Being reminded of them now, however, said in no uncertain terms that he could make my life miserable if I continued writing the book without his and the other elementals' permission. Having survived three attempts to do so that summer, I was not eager to undergo another lesson.

The leprechaun, reliving my memories with me, could see that I was still not happy with his decision, even if I would no longer attempt to override it. Trying a different approach, he said, "Don't focus on what we're not doing. Turn your attention to what we are doing and what we've given both you and others in this book. We've changed your life for the better, wouldn't you say?" He looked at me with his most charming smile.

"Do you mean other than the fact that I have the ongoing costs of tea, toast, and the occasional glass of wine that I can't recoup?" I was starting to forgive him grudgingly.

"Oh, but that's a small price to pay for what we've given you and others, such as . . ."—he searched for a choice gem of information and, finding one, said with enthusiasm—"being able to light a fire with your mind."

I smiled, thinking of my most recent experience with mental fire lighting. The year before I had conducted my first public workshop to help people meet their elementals. We were out in the country and it was Halloween night or All Hallows Eve in the Celtic tradition, when the veil between our two worlds opens for contact. The workshop was going very well and people had shared their previous experiences of various kinds of elementals. Some people, like me, could see elementals. Some heard messages and others felt their presence. Many of those at the workshop had already had proof in their life of the existence of elementals but some had not, and everyone looked forward to being further convinced.

Providing proof was a dilemma. I could share my personal experiences, but that might not be enough for some people. Therefore, I was dependent on the elementals' cooperation in converting the "show-me-and-I'll-believe" types.

The evening was cold, clear, and still. We had just finished dinner when my leprechaun friend, who was co-leading the workshop, asked me to tell everyone to dress warmly and come outside. Earlier that day we had collected wood for the bonfire and he now directed us to gather around the wood in a circle. I was wondering what he was up to and was following directions without knowing, as usual, what he intended.

When we had made a circle, he announced: "Tell everyone to visualize creating a fire with their mind."

After ten years of mental firelighting, I have yet to light a fire in this third-dimensional reality. Being unsure of myself, I was very reluctant to set us all up for failure. I was convinced that trying and failing would lead people to disbelieve and it would be better not to attempt anything.

He heard my thought and, refusing to accept no for an answer, insisted, "Do it."

Attempting to overcome my immense doubt, I said to the group with as much conviction as I could muster, "My leprechaun friend wants us to visualize this wood springing into flames. Let's call on the salamanders who are the fire elementals and imagine the fire blazing."

Nothing happened.

More visualizing, everyone concentrating, nothing happening.

I was just about to admit failure once again when one hundred yards away a blazing fire, much larger than ours would have been, sprang into being in the still dark night. Everyone started to hoot and cheer at our success.

"You see," the leprechaun said, "you created the fire. When you manifest, sometimes the universe gives you what you want but in a little different way than you had expected."

The leprechaun watched me as I recalled All Hallows Eve.

"Well," I admitted, "that was a dramatic way to light a fire, and the folks were mightily impressed."

"Yes," he replied, smiling at his ingenuity, "you humans sure like proof. Speaking of proof, how about what we elementals created for those women when you were walking in Britain last year."

The leprechaun was referring to eighteen women whom I'd taken on a nine-day walk to some of the most sacred sites in England. It was May and the hawthorn and bluebells were in full bloom. The forests were magical in their new spring green and elementals were everywhere. Not everyone could see them as I did, but everyone felt their presence. Still, the women wanted proof.

At lunch, the group asked, "Tanis, could we meet our elementals today?"

This was only the second day and my leprechaun friend, who was thoroughly enjoying walking the trail with all those women, said it would be better if we waited for a few days.

"Could you wait a few days?" I replied to the group.

"The bluebells and forest are so beautiful, couldn't we do it now?" one of the women requested. I could tell by the eager faces that she spoke for all.

Overhearing, the leprechaun said to me, "Well, we could probably arrange something. Tell everyone to stay near you as you set off after lunch."

I repeated his instructions and people could hardly eat quickly enough in anticipation of the gift they would soon receive. Putting on our packs, we started walking in a kind of loose single file down the trail. It was very beautiful and wonderfully magical.

After a half-hour or so of walking in silence, in preparation for this special event, the leprechaun said to me, "Around the next corner is where we want you to stop with the group."

I repeated his words, indicating by the tone of my voice how lucky we were. Everyone walked even more quietly and rounding the corner we entered a dark clearing with no grass and not one bluebell or hawthorn to be seen. The leprechaun could not have picked a sadder, more depressing place. Glancing at the disappointed faces in the group, I knew I was not alone with that thought. I could have moved the group to a more romantic spot, but I'd come to trust my friend's quirky humor and realized that some higher purpose must be in store.

"Everyone sit in a circle," I directed the women.

"No," the leprechaun corrected me, "sit in a horseshoe and keep the top side open where the elemental elders will stand to address you."

I quickly corrected my message to the group and they reordered themselves into the new shape on the dirt. The place was not even flat and some of the women were sloped so precariously that I hoped they weren't going to topple backwards.

"This had better be good," I thought, trying to keep my skepticism in check and, looking up, saw an entourage of all kinds of elementals standing at the top of the horseshoe in the place we had just vacated. There were elves, faeries, dwarves, and with them an old, old leprechaun with a white beard carrying a staff and wearing a white robe.

"Welcome," the old one greeted us. "Each of you is here to meet an elemental with whom to work in order to manifest your gifts in the world. We are committing to work with you, and we expect the same commitment from you. This is something not to be done lightly and, if you cannot commit, you will not receive an elemental with whom to work."

I repeated the old leprechaun's words to the women and, as he spoke, I witnessed an elemental position himself or herself in front of each human. I was filled with joy at how many relationships between elementals and humans were being forged that day. Elementals can sense whether we are committed to and believe in them or not and, obviously, all the women had passed the test. These elementals would be able to travel to wherever these women lived in the world, just as my leprechaun did.

The old leprechaun continued, "Extend your left hand and we will place a gift in it that you can manifest in the world. Notice the gift and transfer it into your right hand. Now, using your etheric vision and your will, extend your right hand and MANIFEST your gift in the world."

As the ancient leprechaun stressed the word "manifest," an incredible thing happened. It was a dead calm day. No breeze was stirring, and yet suddenly we heard a loud crack followed by a crash. Opening our eyes we saw, in shocked surprise, that the limb from the tree had fallen across the top of the horseshoe where we had been instructed not to sit. It had fallen directly in front of the elementals.

"This," said the old one, "is the power of manifestation. Think it and it happens, and this is how you will manifest your gifts in the world. And," he added, pointing to the dirt where we sat, "you don't have to be in bluebells and magical forests to manifest. You can do it anywhere, anytime, even in the cities where you live. Remember this."

With those words he disappeared, and we were left to internalize the many gifts we'd just been given. My leprechaun returned to my side and sat down, pleased at how he had orchestrated such "proof" for us.

Now, back in my living room in Vancouver, the leprechaun waited for me to fully appreciate all the exciting, fun, sharing times we'd had together over the past ten years. Suddenly I realized that our story doesn't end. Time, for him, has no beginning, middle, or end as we humans experience. I recalled how he said that they didn't have books in their world or any need of them because they could access any time and any place they wished. Here I was trying to write a book adapted to human standards with an appropriate ending. Finally I understood that this book—his story as much as mine—was totally in keeping with who he and the elementals are. They are storytellers giving us their experiences in the format of a book, because that's the human way of learning, not theirs.

I was brought back from my reflections by a gruff, "What about the pancakes?" My friend was eyeing the blueberry batter that I'd been making when he arrived.

"I guess everything happens in its right time," I said in acceptance, smiling at the leprechaun as I rose to start the pancakes.

"You're finally learning," he answered. "And don't forget the tea."

(TO BE CONTINUED ?)

Appendix

TEN WAYS FOR HUMANS
TO WORK WITH ELEMENTALS

1. Believe in elementals. Human belief strengthens elementals and gives them energy.
2. Be happy and enthusiastic. Elementals are not attracted to depressed, sad humans.
3. Go to healthy places in nature as often as possible. Walk in forests, along the seashore, lie in a meadow, listen to birds, sit by a brook. Enter into the right vibration of the Earth and listen to what it wants. Humans will purify their vibrations if they do these things.
4. Appreciate the beauty in nature. When humans do this, elementals will be attracted to you.
5. Cooperate and create with nature by planting trees, growing flowers, feeding the birds.
6. Send energy to elementals, who look after trees, flowers, water, and mountains, to keep them healthy. Do this with joy and gratitude.
7. Teach other humans to appreciate nature. Do it with love and joy, and these humans will begin to understand the Earth's needs.
8. Do things spontaneously; free yourself from overplanning and organizing.
9. Take time every day to do nothing. Create a space in both your house and head so magic can occur.
10. In order to contact an elemental who wants to work with you on an ongoing basis, sit in a quiet natural place, close your eyes, and call this elemental to you. Notice what kind of elemental has come. Ask it what its gift is and its name. Listen to this elemental on an ongoing basis; act on its suggestions, and your relationship will become stronger.

TEN WAYS FOR ELEMENTALS
TO WORK WITH HUMANS

1. Do not prejudge all humans as bad but examine each human to find the good in them.
2. Having found the spark of good, breathe your energy into it to enlarge it.
3. When a human pays attention to a plant, tree, or stone, tell him or her what the plant or tree would like in order to be healthier. Even if humans don't hear the message consciously, they will receive it subconsciously.
4. When you see a human who is trying to help nature, cluster around that human and give them all the help you can. Often humans don't think to ask you directly, but our higher selves ask this.
5. Play with humans so that they can recover their childlike joy and wonder. Many humans are depressed and need the joy elementals bring.
6. Give humans proof of your existence. Humans are more inclined to believe in elementals if you do this.
7. Appreciate human strengths of forgiveness, love, persistence, and focus. By associating with humans, elementals will learn these qualities.
8. To body elementals: don't give up. Keep moving your human hosts into situations to catalyze positive change.
9. Don't judge humans by elemental standards. Presently, humans eat beings that live, excrete waste, and age. Through this path we learn to be creators of form and worlds.
10. Surprise us.

ELEMENTAL GUIDELINES
FOR MANIFESTING

1. Humans, from the beginning of their evolution, have been training to become creators—gods-in-training. (p. 16)
2. If humans could raise their vibration and see the lighter vibrations and life force in all living things, they wouldn't be harming the world the way they have been, killing streams, trees, and other life forms. (p. 20)
3. Elementals can manifest whatever they want because, unlike humans, they don't doubt that they can. (p. 21)
4. Humans can hurt elementals just by the force of their will and what they say and do. (p. 21)
5. As humans become more conscious, they become lighter and more porous. (p. 23)
6. Humans don't think they're very good at manifesting. They believe that they have to work hard to get enough food to eat, a place to live, and clothes to wear. (p. 42)
7. Believe that you have the capability to manifest, even though you live in a denser realm, where it is more difficult. (p. 42)
8. All your thoughts about what you want create a reality in other dimensions. These thoughts could easily be brought into third-dimensional form if you weren't so busy canceling them out by sending two conflicting messages to the universe, such as "I would like such and such, but I don't think I can have it because I don't have enough money or education or because someone else has it." Such contradictory messages cancel out the manifestation. (pp. 42-43)
9. Elementals think about what they would like and extend their senses to see it and feel it, and then it appears, because they believe that it will work. (p. 43)

10. Manifestation uses up energy. The older or stronger elementals become, the better able they are to manifest what they want because they have more energy to put into it. (p. 43)

11. What appears to be solid in third-dimensional form consists mostly of space or ether. Elementals have a better understanding and working knowledge of ether and can thereby travel in time and manifest things with comparative ease. (p. 44)

12. The principles for manifesting and demanifesting are the same. (p. 45)

13. Elemental manifestations generally do not have as much life force and substance as items manifested in third-dimensional reality. (p. 46) However, elementals often manifest qualities in other dimensions that can be perceived and experienced in third-dimensional reality—such as sparkle, zest, and other beautifying essences. (p. 43)

14. Realize that many of the limitations of what we think we can do in this human, third-dimensional world are imaginary.

15. Fight discontent with perceived "human limitations" by enjoying and expressing the elemental kingdom's gifts of laughter, joy, curiosity, and enthusiasm—this attracts other humans and opens them to those qualities in themselves. (p. 56)

16. Believe that you can do much more than you have thought possible. You can manifest almost anything that you want. This is an awesome power, but to do this you must improve your powers of concentration. (p. 56)

17. Fear added to conscience results in never taking chances in your life. (p. 56)

18. Elementals work together to hold thoughts and to increase the power of each other's manifestation. Work to improve your powers of concentration, of holding a thought, and of group thought, to increase the power of each other's manifestation. (p. 57)

19. The strength of the mind and the strength of the will are the keys to manifesting for all beings. Humans exist in a denser reality than elementals, so this is why you must work physi-

cally as well as with the mind to manifest what you would like. On the whole, human minds are stronger than the minds of elementals because, to manifest anything, humans need to overcome the resistance of their denser reality, using their will power. This kind of resistance strengthens humans. Unfortunately, there are many humans who are weak-minded and follow others' thoughts and feelings. They don't learn to exert their own mind because it requires more effort. . . . There are many more humans than elementals who are not manifesting their potential. Humans are too passive. But the humans who do manifest are a great deal stronger than almost all elementals, if they only knew it. (pp. 64-65)

20. By keeping an image strongly in mind, a farmer usually gets what was imagined, but still needs to work with nature to plant the seed. Humans could create wonderful food, beautiful gardens, and healthy trees if they listened to what nature wanted, as well as having the ability to visualize it happening. (pp. 65-66)

21. In the human mystical tradition there are twelve rays of power that create our world, and to become a creator each of us must learn to use the gifts of each of these rays. Five of these rays (such as rose) are unmanifested, meaning that their gift is to dissolve or eliminate what is no longer needed in the world. (p. 118)

22. A shamrock has got four petals, indicating balance of the four main elements in nature—earth, air, fire, and water. (p. 118) Fire is the highest of the elements. You have fire in your body that humans call kundalini energy. This kundalini energy carries the divine life force of the Creator through a central energy channel that runs up your spinal cord. This channel is connected to the seven major energy centers in your body that you call chakras. The kundalini fire nourishes these chakras which in turn energize all your organs to which the chakras are connected. Even your blood carries the life force of fire energy. Fire is needed to manifest what you want in both of our

worlds. It is the spark that triggers every manifestation. (pp. 119-20)

23. Control of all four elements must be mastered in order to be a well-balanced creator who can create a world. This is what the being who created this planet, the one you call God, has done. But fire is the most important element, as it is needed to create things quickly in your third-dimensional world. (p. 121)

24. Humans must strike a balance between the water and fire elements. The gift of water is one of peace and tranquility, of being, not doing. . . . Water is the conductor through which the elements of fire, air, and earth move. (p. 122)

25. Air/ether is the space within all matter. By controlling air, both humans and elementals can travel in space, time, and between dimensions. Air is a by-product of space or ether. (p. 124)

26. What you visualize takes place in the ethers. Humans have no idea that every thought they think makes a record in the ethers. The stronger the thought, the stronger the record. If humans imagined clean water and healthy forests and called on the elementals of these places to help, they could restore health to this planet in no time. (p. 136)

27. One person working with the divine will affect thousands of people who are not. . . . Humans are changing. We must visualize the way they are becoming and not collapse into the old image of what they have been. (p. 136)

28. Masters must learn the laws of polarity and working with the electromagnetic currents of the earth to move between dimensions and in space and time. (p. 143)

29. The Earth provides the raw material for humans to work with in learning to become creators. (p. 144) The earth element is needed to create form. (p. 143)

30. Your etheric body works in the fourth dimension and it has accomplished what you asked it to do. However there is great resistance in your mind to believe that you can accomplish this in your third-dimensional reality. Even as you visualize yourself doing it, part of your mind is saying it can't do it. (p. 146)

Further Reading

Colum, Padric, *A Treasury of Irish Folklore,* Crown Publishers, New York, 1954.

Evans-Wentz, W. Y., *The Fairy-Faith in Celtic Countries,* University Books, New York, 1966. (First published in 1911.)

Findhorn Community, *The Findhorn Garden,* Harper and Row, New York, NY, 1975.

Gettings, Fred, *The Salamander Tales,* Floris Books, Edinburgh, 1981.

Gregory, Lady, *Visions and Beliefs in the West of Ireland,* Gerrards Cross, Snythe, 1970.

MacLean, Dorothy, *To Hear the Angels Sing,* Lorian Press, 1980.

MacManus, Diarmuid, *Irish Earth Folk,* The Devin-Adair Company, New York, 1959.

McGowan, Hugh, *Leprechauns, Legends and Irish Tales,* Victor Gollancz Ltd., London, 1988.

Roads, Michael, *Journey into Nature,* H J Kramer Inc., Tiburon, CA, 1990.

Small Wright, Machelle, *Behaving As If the God in All Life Mattered,* Perelandra, Warrenton, VA, 1987.

Von Gilder, Dora, *Fairies,* Quest Books, Wheaton, IL, 1994.

Yeats, W.B., *Irish Fairy and Folk Tales,* Modern Library, NY, 1893.

About the Author

ANIS HELLIWELL, M.ED., author of *Decoding Destiny: Keys to Mankind's Spiritual Evolution,* is a student and teacher of the inner mysteries, living in Vancouver, Canada. Since 1985 she has led people from all over the world on tours to sacred sites in Egypt, Israel, Peru, Bolivia, India, Nepal, France, Britain, Scotland, Ireland, the American Southwest, and New Zealand.

Since childhood, she has seen and heard elementals, angels, spirit guides, and master teachers on other planes. For sixteen years she has conducted a therapy practice and seminars internationally to help people with their spiritual transformation.

In addition to her spiritual workshops, she has worked since 1976 as a consultant to businesses, universities, and government, both to create healthy organizations and to help people develop their personal and professional potential. Her clients include IBM, C.B.C., Institute of Chartered Accountants, World Business Academy, David Suzuki Foundation, Ministry of Fisheries and Oceans, University of Calgary, Banff Centre for Management, Alberta Medical Association, and World Future Society.

In both her corporate and spiritual work, she is committed to helping people to develop right relationships with themselves, others, and the Earth.

To write to the author, order books and tapes, or for information on upcoming tours and workshops, please contact:

Tanis Helliwell Corporation
156 Hamptons Landing N.W.
Calgary, Alta. T3A 5R5 Canada
Toll Free: 1-800-745-4779 Tel: 403-241-0933
Email: info@iitransform.com
Website: www.tanishelliwell.com

~~~~~

Decoding Destiny: Keys to Mankind's Spiritual Evolution
US $13.00 (CDN $18.00)

AUDIO CASSETTES:

Series A—Discovering Yourself
Guided visualizations on both sides
1. Path of Your Life / Your Favourite Place
2. Eliminating Negativity / Purpose of Your Life
3. Linking Up World Servers / Healing the Earth

Series B - The Inner Mysteries
Lectures on side A and guided visualizations on side B
1. Reawakening Ancestral Memory / Between the Worlds
2. The Celtic Mysteries / Quest for the Holy Grail
3. The Egyptian Mysteries / Initiation in the Pyramid of Giza
4. The Greek Mysteries / Your Male and Female Archetypes
5. The Christian Mysteries / Jesus' Life: A Story of Initiation

Individual audio cassettes US $12.00 (CDN $16.00)
Series A (3 tapes)—US $30 (CDN $40)
Series B (5 tapes)—US $55 (CDN $70)

VIDEO CASSETTES:

1. Take Your Soul to Work
2. Managing the Stress of Change
Individual video cassettes US $28.00 (CDN $39.00)

Prices and Handling

Individual Tapes: $16 Cdn/$12 US
Series A (5 tapes): $70 Cdn/$55 US
Series B (3 tapes): $40 Cdn/$30 US
Postage: to $18-$5; $19-$100-**$10**; over $100-**$15**
Canadian Sales: add 7% GST & 7% PST for B.C.